Herding Dog

Their Origins and Development in Britain

Iris Combe

faber and faber

LONDON · BOSTON

First published in 1987
by Faber and Faber Limited
3 Queen Square, London WC1N 3AU
Photoset and printed in Great Britain by
Redwood Burn Ltd Trowbridge Wiltshire

All rights reserved

© Iris Combe 1987

British Library Cataloguing in Publication Data

Combe, Iris
  Herding dogs.
  1. Sheep dogs – Great Britain
  I. Title
  636.7'3   SF428.6
  ISBN 0–571–14715–1

This book is dedicated to the memory of Tom, whose great courage and special sense of humour enriched each venture we undertook

Contents

Illustrations

Illustrations

Preface

If I did not occasionally indulge in a romantic outlook, I doubt if I could come to terms with the harsh, cruel and sometimes unjust realities of rural living. Life with a herding dog brings to the pastoral scene a strange mixture of moods, ranging from loneliness and tranquillity to persistent struggle against the elements. Together the herdsman and his dog can be found ready to accept nature's challenge at every season, when the early summer haze lifts from the water meadows or the swirling mists and raging storms of winter vanish over the mountains.

1   James Bourchier, the author's great-uncle, who was a correspondent for *The Times* in Bulgaria for over 25 years, made an extensive study of the evolution and history of herding dogs as a hobby. He lived most of the time in the hills with local shepherds.

   The portrait by Michailomy (1908) which now hangs in the Board room of *The Times* shows Bourchier in traditional shepherd's dress with a local shepherding dog by his side.

   He became a national hero and a set of stamps was issued in his honour in 1924; his shrine is in Rilo Monastery in the hills above Sophia.

   Photo: The Times

Herding Dogs

The fluctuating status of the herdsman on the social ladder has had a direct bearing on the development of his dogs, depending upon which rung he has found himself at a given moment in time. Shepherding is not just an occupation but a way of life with all its ups and downs and special social requirements. I thank God I was born and raised in the country for it has given me a greater understanding of the simple philosophy of those involved with livestock farming, together with a sympathetic appreciation of their struggles and of rural life in general. The memories of the country characters who have helped to further my education, and the unusual situations in which I have found myself, came flooding back as I compiled each chapter of this book.

Country folk hold no academic qualifications, all their knowledge and wisdom come from practical experience. For me, the roadside was an early if impromptu classroom. At home in Ireland I would often sit listening to a band of gypsy urchins squabbling and bragging about their poaching exploits. From them I gained an entirely new perception of the hunter and the hunted. I can still recall mixed feelings of shame, guilt, bravado and confusion when I was caught on an expedition with these children, just as a small boy was aiming his catapult with deadly accuracy at a distant target. These were not scenes from some Romany romance; this was live opera and I had joined the chorus with my vocal chords fully stretched.

I doubt, too, if any teacher of natural history could have made the subject as interesting as the old ploughman to whom I sometimes took what he called his 'progings' (the original ploughman's lunch of a cottage loaf, a huge lump of cheese and a pickled onion, washed down by cold tea, beer or cider according to taste). He taught me the art of quiet observation. We would sit in total silence on a bank or a fallen tree while he munched and pointed his finger in the direction of anything of interest. Suddenly his horse and dog would raise their heads and quiver their nostrils in alarm; the animals in the hedgerows froze in their tracks. While they decided on their next move, we could see a fox streaking across the fresh ploughed furrows, and minutes later we would hear a huntsman and his hounds drawing in a nearby covert.

Dogs and children are renowned for breaking down social barriers and drawing naturally shy people into conversation. My husband Tom was also well endowed with this gift which proved invaluable with crusty gamekeepers unable to believe that anyone has honourable intentions, or lone hill shepherds whose one desire is to be left alone by the outside world.

My intention in this study is not only to pass on the knowledge I have accumulated about herdsmen and their dogs, but to highlight some of the political or social events and rural happenings which have led to the integration of the herdsmen's way of life and the life-style of the landowners who employed them. As we shall see, it was the wealth created by the Industrial Revolution and the environment of the English country estates that led to the emergence of our present-day pedigree-registered breeds and all the leisure activities connected with owning a shepherding dog.

I am deeply conscious that not all who read this book will agree with my sentiments, but I have been guided by a desire to give fuller recognition to the herdsmen of Britain and their dogs who have contributed so much to our precious heritage. I would like my book to be regarded as a special tribute to them.

1

A Heritage Collection

This book is not just a history of a special kind of dog, it is an arrangement of unique recollections about a way of life recounted to me by country folk, old-tyme hill and forest shepherds, drovers, graziers and others closely connected with the pastoral scene. It is important that such accounts should be written down, for as these great characters of the shepherding world fade out, together with the tools of their trade, so too does a part of our national heritage.

When one is searching for a missing link in some research, nothing is more frustrating than to be told, 'If only you could have spoken to "old so-and-so" he could have given you the right answer, what a pity he died last week!' for all too often no one will know what happened to all his interesting and valuable books or other items. These are regular occurrences and such a tragic waste. There is a limit, too, to the length of time memorabilia can be retained without being committed to paper before becoming confused and finally valueless. When this happens, searching for the historical accuracy of these accounts or recollections can be a mammoth task. No modern invention can yet replace a modern shepherd's dog, and so the art of training these dogs lives on, but increasingly sophisticated technology, developments in the world economy and changing tastes and life-styles are all having their effect on the pattern of livestock farming. Time may be running out for our herding breeds as it already has for many other types of livestock, though some, like the farm horses, have adapted well to new roles.

My most treasured antique collection is an assortment of boxes and parcels containing books, pictures, photographs, newspaper cuttings and other mementoes all connected – sometimes quite remotely – with the pastoral scene, shepherding life and herding dogs. I started this collection in my childhood and for a long time it remained gathering dust in our loft. Then a few years ago we had to move to a smaller house, and a big 'clear-out' of anything unnecessary was essential. However, an awful feeling of nostalgia engulfed us when the dreaded area of the loft had to be tackled and my husband asked me what I intended to do with what he called my 'Heritage Collection'.

His suggestion was that I should put all the worthwhile information into a book and consign the rest to the bonfire. I have been told by friends who have shared my interest, and by people who have come to me for information on some past event, that my collection was of great historical interest and value, so I greeted the idea of taking up Tom's challenge with enthusiasm. The more I thought about the eventual destination of my collection, the more the idea of a book appealed to me. The big question now was whether I had the courage, confidence and time to put all this material in some order of sequence.

It was only when I began to sort through the material, dividing the references or photographs of the various breeds from those of the shepherding events that I realized the full extent of the variety of herding types of breed. I think the true inspiration for this book began here.

Antiquarian books have always had a fatal attraction for me and antiquarian dog books form the main part of my collection, but the choice is very limited; these books are difficult to find and very expensive. The shelves of present-day bookshops, on the other hand, are weighed down by books, both large and small, devoted to recording the merits and progress of various breeds of dog since they became exhibits in the show ring or participants in trials. However, in the majority of these canine books written after 1873 when organized shows and trials began, only a few pages, or at most a chapter on early history or origin – not always accurate – preface the know-how of breeding, showing and general care.

Beautifully bound volumes on the history and origins of all manner of farm livestock abound in public libraries and private collections, but old works devoted solely to the dogs and their masters directly involved in the management of such livestock are sadly lacking, at any rate until Scotland was joined to the English crown. Soon after this momentous event writers, painters and musicians began to extol the beauty, romance and mystery of Scotland. Mendelssohn captured all the moods of the islands in his Hebridean overture ('Fingal's Cave'), while Landseer and Ansdell brought Scottish scenes to life on canvas, and the pens of Sir Walter Scott, Robert Burns and others recorded never to be forgotten events and interesting people. However, it is to the writings of James Hogg, known as the Etterick shepherd, that most canine historians refer, and it was through Hogg that the collie or shepherd's dog of Scotland earned a popular image which had never been afforded to English shepherds and their dogs.

Many years ago I noticed in a Sotheby's catalogue that some original letters of James Hogg to Lord Byron were coming up for sale. My curiosity aroused, I went to the view day to read the contents. These letters gave me an interesting insight into Hogg's character, hopes and aspirations. In one paragraph he pleads with Byron to exert his influence on his publishers to get some of his own poems published. He indicates that he wrote on shepherding matters and about his father's dogs out of boredom, and because it was the only subject of which he had any experience. In fact, like Robert Burns, Hogg was a failure as a farmer and, also like Burns, was advised by his father to concentrate on literary talents; the value of this advice has been reaped for posterity.

I suspect that like many others, I had presumed from reading Hogg's shepherding stories that he was in fact an authority on herding dogs, as indeed his father must have been, but even though this is not the case, his writings do give us a most valuable insight into a shepherd's life on the southern uplands of Scotland.

The richest source of pastoral history and memorabilia lies in Wales. Visitors to the Principality can sometimes purchase delightful and informative locally published books on a number of subjects, but as a rule, unless one is on very good terms with the folk of the valleys or knows the Welsh language, the material is as difficult to obtain as the coal from the mines. In Ireland, the land of my birth, literature on old farming dogs is non-existent, but as I grew up there, free as a mountain hare and equally wild, the farm dogs and the country folk were my close friends and an integral part of my education. I experienced the pastoral scene at the grass roots, although my researches have of necessity been confined to old farming records.

Searching through the histories of our great country houses, and studying the management of their estates, I found a tremendous amount of information on domestic livestock and agricultural progress, but almost no reference to the dogs connected with the management of these animals. In the histories of the Bakewells of Leicester, for example, famous for their experimental breeding of sheep and cattle, and of the Cokes of

Holkham Hall in Norfolk, a family who contributed so much to advance agriculture and livestock breeding (it was in Holkham that the famous sheep shearings known as Coke's clippings took place), there is no mention of their herding dogs. There are only a few brief references to the shepherds and their dogs at Woburn Abbey and one or two other large estates where extensive livestock breeding and rearing produced the means of upkeep.

This is in contrast with the abundance of ancient and modern literature on sporting dogs. Most of the beautifully illustrated books on canidae in general were produced by professional journalists who were interested mainly in sporting dogs, and could not possibly have been experts in all the breeds they wrote about; instead, they relied upon contributions from authorities on each subject. In the case of the shepherd's dog and other herding or pastoral dogs, the people who had the greatest knowledge on the subject were very often unable to read or write, and as I know only too well, one has to scrutinize carefully verbal material supplied from these sources, in order to sift the truth from pure nostalgia or romanticizing.

In the past, contributions on rural matters came mainly from clergymen and other country folk interested in the literary arts as well as from self-opinionated journalists who happened upon the pastoral scene but were not part of it. This may account for the confusing descriptions and the various names given to the same type of dog, as I discovered when consulting the index in some of these old volumes, which frequently referred one to the wrong page, but in some instances led me to some new and exciting information. This indicated to me that references by modern authors to the contents of some of the old volumes had not been personally researched, or had been taken out of context and therefore had little value.

With so little antiquarian literature available on the subject of herding dogs, authors have to clutch at straws, and in some cases the contributions in these old volumes had in any case only the very remotest connection with the subject. They were also frequently written in jocular vein, and humour, especially when it belongs to a particular period, offers different interpretations to its readers. In fact there is only one thing one can be sure of when writing about canine matters and that is that one is bound to be challenged at some point, as so much is a matter of speculation and personal opinion.

I once mentioned this in conversation with Clifford Hubbard (affectionately known as Doggie Hubbard), one of our most important collectors of canine history. I shall not repeat his rather unflattering remarks about modern authors, but he wagged his finger at me and told me to read up all those old books for myself lest I be tarred with the same brush. Clifford, whose own books on working dogs of the world are always in great demand, told me that when he was researching for one of his publications he spent six months camping in the grounds of the University of Wales in order to visit the library each day. Unfortunately domestic commitments did not allow me the privilege of such dedication or concentration, but I took his advice and travelled to London on a number of occasions to study various historical books in the British Library.

On one occasion while sorting out the newspaper cuttings in my collection I came across a number of forgotten articles and letters to the editors of *The Field* expressing opinions or giving reports of sheepdog sales, trials and matters of management. Feeling that this might provide a useful source of information, I wrote to the editor asking for any information on the subject of sheepdogs. This alone is an indication of my naivety at the time. I received a polite letter back saying the editor was not quite sure exactly what kind of information I required, but I was most welcome to search through their archives. It was not a surprising conclusion on his part for although I had been collecting and researching material for a number of years, I did not know myself at that stage exactly which line I was pursuing. However, his offer was too tempting to miss.

A friend came with me to London to explore *The Field* archives. As it was just after the war, in 1947, I think the entrance to the cellars was still protected by sandbags against bomb blast and flooding and the collection of weekly issues dating back to 1853 were stacked on very high shelving protected by a curtain of cobwebs. Brushing these aside and dodging the scaffolding supporting the roof, we searched the indexes of as many volumes as we could reach for anything remotely connected with collies, sheep or dogs, and my friend took notes as I read the letters, reports or articles that seemed of interest. Although we looked and felt like potholers when we emerged the adventure was well worth while; the contents of the articles and letters confirmed a great deal of the information given to me over the years by retired people in the shepherding world which I had up to then suspected of simply being rather inaccurate reminiscences, and several of these I later followed up.

Of course, no amount of historical research can compare with the knowledge gained through personal contacts with those having a lifelong connection in their profession or calling, but this is not something that can be added to a material collection, so in order to be made widely available all these notes and experiences have to be written down. I have been fortunate enough to have travelled a fair amount with my husband both in Britain and abroad, and to have had the privilege of staying with families who owned or worked herding dogs or were interested in the breeds.

Country folk the world over are reserved by nature, but open up when overseas visitors are about. I have learned so much from these 'international' gatherings while sitting round huge kitchen tables laden with local delicacies, or sipping weird concoctions on patios or terraces. I have the gift of the gab and also that of being able to feel happy and at ease in any company, both of which have stood me in good stead on such occasions. Among Tom's many gifts was that of striking the right note to encourage others to talk, and being a good listener. Language barriers seemed no problem at these gatherings. Faded photographs, family mementoes, newspaper cuttings, rosettes and trophies displayed with pride, all tell the tale of the pattern of family life on the local pastoral scene. I hope that my readers will experience as much enjoyment from reading this blend of history and personal recollections as I have had from gathering it all. For there is no doubt in my mind that although many of our herding breeds have disappeared, been altered or taken on new roles, as valuable and cared for companions or show dogs in some instances, the majority of the owners of this new race of herding dogs want to learn more about their original role and ancestry before it evaporates into the mists of time, as so much of it has done already.

2

The Status of Shepherds
and the Role of their Dogs

There are two generally accepted beliefs regarding the pastoral scene which are misleading to say the least, and upon which I would like to direct a different if not altogether new light. The first concerns the original status of the shepherds and the kind of people they were, and the second the purpose for which their dogs were trained. The training of a dog was to assist him in the struggle for survival, but as man became more civilized the purpose for which a dog was trained depended upon its trainer's status, rank or calling. It is always presumed that shepherds were in fact sheep keepers or herdsmen and that their dogs were herding dogs, but this is not always the case.

The shepherd's status

The position of a shepherd in social or political history needs to be distinguished from that in rural history. In social history he ranked as a leader of the tribe, which was the original meaning of the word 'shepherd', and as such he was in constant need of protection from enemies among his fellow men, and from wild beasts; the role of his dog was that of bodyguard and hunter. In political history a gentleman or even a king could claim the status of a shepherd, the hawk, horse and dog being symbols of such status necessary to their rank or way of life.

John Speed (1552–1629) was a man who knew the worth of wool for he was brought up in the tailoring trade and became a member of the Merchant Taylors Company in 1614. In his leisure hours he studied the life-styles of people in high places and wrote *The History of Great Britain under the Conquests of Ye Romans, Saxons, Danes, Normans, with the Successions, Lives, Acts and Issues of English Monarchs, from Julius Caesar to our most gracious Sovereigne King James*, to give the full title. This was first published in 1611 with a second publication in 1614. In 1627 came a third publication, but this time under the title of *A Capital Continuation of the Theatre of the Empire of Great Britaine*.

We learn a great deal from John Speed's work about social customs during successive occupations of our islands. For instance he tells that when Edward the Elder died in 924 he had had three wives, and the first, named Egwina, was the daughter of a shepherd. He goes on to explain that 'she was the daughter of a gentleman, perhaps a country gentleman, but not a soldier, and in the language of the Court he was called a Shepherd.'

In fact, in both social and political history one frequently comes across references to this rank of 'shepherd'. Members of noble or aristocratic families, from at least medieval times, when not following a military career, were supposed to be employed in the breeding of sheep, which were a natural source of wealth to landowner and crown alike. Particular attention and concessions were granted to those engaged in this brand of animal husbandry.

In medieval times the eldest son, and others who were physically fit, were expected to follow a naval or military career, while the less fit took up the arts, gentle sports, astrology or other academic studies, or became merchants. The youngest boy in the family, however, was always referred to as the 'shepherd boy' and was expected to follow an agricultural career to help with the management of the estates. This privilege of choice did of course depend upon the social class to which the family belonged, but jobs for the boys in any family have always been a universal problem.

Turning to the status of a shepherd in rural history, the word is a corruption of sheep-herdsman, and as such the shepherd ranked low on the social scale. On the other hand, keepers of livestock might range from owners of flocks or herds to head hired herdsmen. The occupation or calling of these men and women – for many women were employed in sheep rearing in the past – may have been humble, but they possessed more wisdom and practical knowledge about every aspect of rural life than did the academics who wrote about them, their dogs or their way of life.

The contribution our shepherding families of the past made to the English economy was incalculable, as agriculture, livestock rearing and particularly the wool trade had for centuries been as important a source of income to those who owned land as it was to the national coffers. However, the herdsmen generally received little credit or recognition except in times of wars, natural disasters or unusual rural happenings.

The Plague or Black Death of 1348/50 was one such disaster which first gave prominence to those who worked on the land and highlighted their true value. The disease wiped out one-third of the population, and hired labour, both in industry and on the land, became scarce. For the first time this gave labourers worthy of their hire real bargaining power. Unions had already been formed to safeguard the interests of those in industry, but up to that time, the only bargaining power available to the herdsman was his own initiative or experience.

Following the Black Death, much good cultivated land and many good livestock strains were neglected as a result of illness or the shortage of hired labour. Wealthy landlords who survived the plague bought up farms or parcels of neglected land, and long before the Enclosure Act came into being, they started to farm more intensively in the form of enclosures. This called for a higher standard of animal husbandry and required less labour to look after it. Skilled herdsmen were in great demand. Head keepers and herdsmen got the recognition they deserved and shepherds once more became men of consequence.

How one classifies the next major historical event to affect the shepherd's status depends upon which side of the Border one was born, for this was the Union between England and Scotland in 1707, and a real milestone in shepherding history as well. For some considerable time after the Union an intense hatred of the English was the mark of a true Scot, but this did not prevent him from accepting the Sassenach's cash, even if in some cases it meant leaving the homeland.

So it was that for almost a century, with little employment in the rural areas of Scotland, shepherds and their families came over the Border to take up responsible situations on the big estates in England – and of course most brought their dogs too. These hard-working and efficient Scotsmen and their dogs made such an impression on English landowners that they began to dominate the pastoral scene and it became something of a status symbol to employ a Scot as head shepherd and his wife or one of his family as head cook or housekeeper.

The role of the shepherd's dog

As long ago as Roman Britain, the independent hill shepherds and their families were held in high regard, the location of their farms and the versatility of their dogs being of great assistance in supplying and making contacts with hill forts, and in watching mountain passes. A few older-generation hill shepherds I

have spoken to in the North of England are convinced that the
ancestry of some of today's hill dogs can be traced back to
Roman times, and this is not beyond the bounds of possibility
when one compares the lighter conformation of our hill dogs of
the past with those heavier, slower types working on lower
meadows.

The fortifications built for the defence of the whole of the
Roman Empire, of which Britain was regarded as a western
extension, involved ingenious supply systems, especially in
mountain ranges, and for this purpose other types of herding,
guarding or shepherd's dogs were evolved for special tasks.
The remains of Hadrian's Wall, stretching from the Tyne to the
Solway, is still one of the reminders to us today of these fortifications, with its many built-in forts. Those of Maiden Castle in
Dorset were of great importance too, and many skeletons of
dogs have been found in the ruins, though unfortunately we
can only speculate about the purpose for which they were used.

Military supplies to mountain forts, both here and on the
Continent, were provided by the army and brought up by mule
or pack-horse in suitable weather, but the daily rations came
from local farming families. In darkness or when snow or mists
obliterated the paths or tracks, only a dog drawing a small cart
could get through. A dog could also warn a lone sentry of
impending danger, and when he needed help a message was
attached to the dog's collar before he was despatched for home.
The reward of a good meal for the dog at either end of its
journey usually encouraged a quick passage once it had learned
the route. Some of the soldiers and their families lived all their
lives in these forts, often becoming part-time herdsmen, and
assisted by these hill shepherds' dogs.

When taxes in Britain were paid in wheat, local peasant families grew extra to stock the granaries of the forts, and they also
earned extra money by supplying the troops with other rations
from domestic animals kept for their own use. The breeding

and training of dogs to guard the flocks, homesteads and forts were also a source of extra income. The powers of endurance and scenting abilities of these dogs were quite exceptional. These elderly shepherds would also often use a goat brought up in the house from a kid for herding or gathering the small flocks, sheep being compulsive followers.

It is a generally accepted belief that the training of a dog to herd was a natural progression from training to guard, but this is not in fact the case – at least not in Britain. As the threat to man from the larger wild beasts diminished, so did the need for the original shepherds' mastiffs, these fierce, vociferous, powerful creatures, loyal only to their masters, like the legendary Gelert belonging to Llewellyn, King of Wales. Dogs such as these would have maimed or at least stampeded flocks or herds. A smaller, less aggressive type of guard which accepted more discipline and to which the farm animals could get accustomed, was the original herdsman's dog.

In the *Sportsman's Cabinet*, vol. 1 (1803) I found an exceptionally good account of the training of this type of dog to protect flocks, which was witnessed by Charles Darwin on one of his tours to South America. On this occasion Darwin noted that large flocks of sheep were being guarded by dogs at a great distance from any house or other dwelling. He discovered that these dogs had been specially trained for the task. The method the flockmaster followed was to hold a ewe a few times a day for a pup to suck, and to make a nest for it from the sheep's wool. At no time was the pup allowed to associate with other dogs or other people, so that eventually it had no wish to leave the flock and thus its guarding instincts were fully exploited. Next, the pup was trained to come to the house at certain times each day for meat, the sheep would follow him, and in this way he was trained to lead the flocks back to the folds or yards.

Difficulties sometimes occurred when a young pup wanted to play with the lambs. These dogs grew up quite fierce and neither wild dogs nor wolves would attack a flock guarded by them. I have also read an account of a similar procedure in a book of ancient traditions in the Lammermuir Hills in Scotland. Both describe how it was possible to train the flock dogs of the past to guard one group of animals and yet attack others, and so to discriminate between friend or foe – but these were different dogs of different types, conformation and temperament.

Many a modern hill shepherd as well as a lonely sentry from a past era can recall the value of the warmth and companionship his dog has provided and which has often saved his life and sanity when stranded in an isolated hut in appalling weather conditions.

3

Tools of the Trade,
Past and Present

The confidence of those who believe that nothing can replace our herding dogs would be well founded if livestock farming were to continue in its present form, but much as I would like to share such optimism, for almost half a century I have been reading signs and listening to distant rumblings of change which prevent me from doing so.

The majority of farms in the British Isles, especially hill farms where a herding dog is absolutely essential, are small family businesses, but the sheer economics of farming, changing tastes and other restrictions, are forcing many small livestock farmers out of business. The tendency in this day and age is towards intensive livestock breeding and rearing in large enclosed areas where the tools of the trade are most likely to be an array of sophisticated equipment and medication to care for the internal and external well-being of the stock, and, all importantly, to promote a rapid rate of growth.

Today, assemblies sitting in ivory towers are directing the building of mountains of grain and dairy produce and lakes of oil and wine which, like slag heaps and gravel pits, no one knows what to do with. In the face of such policies one wonders how long the small British farmer can survive, and whether, if he goes under, the need for a herding dog will also disappear. This may seem to be dramatizing the situation, but when one realizes how many of our herding breeds or types defined in this chapter have already vanished, I feel it is all the more important to record this very special section of our natural heritage.

Development

The Romans brought us their farming expertise and found in Britain the climatic and economical conditions favourable to livestock farming. Sheep farming and the wool trade became big business during the Roman occupation. Up until that period only slow progress had been made in farming methods and animal husbandry with no significant changes taking place. Now, however, demand was outstripping the supply from the established flocks in pasture, and techniques for the economical management of the wild sheep and goats which roamed our hills and forests with the deer had not yet been developed.

To increase the supply and vary the quality of the fleeces, the Romans imported from North Africa and the Iberian Peninsula sheep and goats which were accustomed to being herded, and in many cases the herdsmen and their dogs accompanied the shipments. A more detailed account of this appears in chapter 12 on Irish collies, and the ancestry of a few of our droving types of the past can also be traced back to these imported dogs.

The threat from wild beasts to the ancient Britons and their livestock was minimal compared to the raids from the Druid settlements, for both human and animal sacrifices. Perhaps this is why the Romans found our mastiffs superior to those in other parts of their empire, and as the necessity for the big shepherds' mastiffs or keepers' dogs diminished, their role became only a supporting one to the new type of herdsman's dog appearing on the pastoral scene. Before we leave the question of the Roman influence, it is worth looking at some interesting and informative remarks in *De Re Rustica*, a farm treatise by Marcus Terentius Varro, who wrote many books on farming matters. 'There are two kinds of dogs, one for hunting with the wild beasts of the wood, and the other trained for the purposes of defence and used by the shepherds.' Varro then goes on to describe the physical qualities of a shepherd's dog for the purpose of defence and suggests ways of accustoming the dog to wearing protective spiked leather collars. Elsewhere he tells us,

> Be careful not to buy dogs from hunters or butchers, for the dogs of butchers are too idle to follow the flock, while hunting dogs, if they see a hare or a stag, will chase after it instead of after the sheep. Thus the best is one that has been bought from a shepherd and has been trained to follow sheep or has had no training at all.
>
> The number of dogs is usually fixed in proportion to the size of the flock, and in most cases it is considered proper for one dog to follow each shepherd. . . . If the district is one in which there is an abundance of wild beasts more dogs will be necessary, and this is the case with those who have to travel with their flock to summer and winter quarters by long tracks through the forest. But for a flock staying at the farmhouse two are considered sufficient, one male and one female. For so they hold better to their work. For the same dog when he has a companion grows keener than before, and if one or other fall ill, the flock need not be without a dog.

The Romans are credited with being the first to classify dogs, which they arranged into three groups according to the purpose for which they were used:

Herding Dogs

Class 1: *Canis villatica* or house dog. We presume that this category included all the types used for human protection and the destruction of vermin around the villas.

Class 2: *Canis pastoralis* or shepherd's dog.

Class 3: *Venatici* or sporting dogs.

This classification indicates that there were sufficient pure or recognizable breeds or types at that period in each of these groups, although they are not individually listed.

Centuries later in his *Histoire naturelle*, published in 1755, the French naturalist Buffon argues that 'all the breeds known [in this day] were descended from the shepherds' dogs and [that] all savage peoples who kept sheep had a sheepdog, and therefore the sheepdog must be the original dog. The sheepdog is the most intelligent of all dogs and must therefore have been domesticated earlier than any other.'

This is a difficult argument to follow, and if it were the case, sheepdogs must have been among the earliest tools of the trade; but we know that savage peoples were hunters, not farmers, and as we have seen, as man became more civilized he exploited the instincts of the dog to fill his larder and help him in the struggle for survival. In this respect he regarded dogs as superior in bodily strength, speed, agility and courage. He found that nature had equipped them better to cope with environmental and climatic conditions and that their senses far exceeded those of the human frame.

The scenting powers of dogs are indeed almost beyond the comprehension of man. Intelligence, memory and understanding, stamina and great physical courage are also part of the valuable genes bank of all canines, but these qualities have been developed to a higher degree in the dogs which work with livestock.

Definitions

Before defining the various types of herding dog, it would be useful to look at their hidden assets or special qualities.

Instinct is a nervous subconscious mental process. Sights, scents and sounds received in the brain from the nose, eyes and ears are instantly processed into natural reflex actions, which differ in each species. There are authorities who suggest that this miraculous, almost simultaneous process signifies reasoning power, while others suggest that dogs do not possess this; although such reactions are a matter of the degree of intelligence the dog displays. One thing is certain, instinct is an inherited quality that can be channelled by man for a specific purpose and is highly developed in herding dogs.

Intelligence in a species is displayed in terms of mental characteristics, instincts and emotions which are the result of breeding by natural selection, and form an established genes pattern. Long association with man, continual training and selective breeding can influence the degree of intelligence displayed in a dog.

Memory: unless a dog is receptive to training and discipline and can then retain or memorize what it has been taught, reacting instinctively and intelligently to these lessons, it is useless for work.

Understanding: complete trust and understanding are essential between a herdsman and his dog. Without these, a dog's memory will retain only any unpleasant associations from its contact with man, which may cause it to become uncooperative to training and to revert to its aggressive instincts.

Temperament: by temperament we mean the character of the dog, a very important quality today in a dog which has to come into contact with so many facets of daily life. In the past correct temperament was judged by physical courage and loyalty. In appearance many of the local strains looked similar, but differed greatly in temperament as well as in stamina and methods of working.

Colour cannot be described as a hidden asset but it does have some importance both for the early guarding types and the herding types past and present, depending on the physical features of the terrain they work in.

The large white breeds that today we call the mountain breeds were the true guards in regions above the snow-line, where their main task was to give warning of approaching danger to the forts or to lone sentries, not to flocks. The colour was excellent camouflage for the dogs as 'undercover agents' but was useless to deter wild animals.

The use of black or brindle dogs proved more successful for the protection of flocks or herds on land bounded by forests or large unfenced grazing areas, black being a colour which instils fear into wild animals. Many of the special attributes of the modern herding dog make him exceedingly useful for mountain rescue work in atrocious weather conditions and hazardous terrain, and black dogs are found to be less prone to snow blindness. Most of the early strains were either all black or black and tan in colour and it is not certain when the white markings became a trade mark of the sheepdog. There are several theories regarding the reason for this addition, and these really belong in the field of genetics, but some possible theories are touched upon in chapter 9.

Groups and nomenclature of our herding dogs

Pastoral dogs

These can be any dogs connected with rural life or used solely in the management of stock on pasture grazing.

Droving dogs

To define droving dogs accurately, other than stating the obvious, would be impossible, for they were a collection of canines of every shape, size, make and colour, each selected by the drover for its natural instincts to deal with a certain breed of livestock being transported, and trained for specific tasks en route.

The requirements of a drover's dog were a stout heart, good lungs, rock-hard feet, great physical courage and a strongly developed instinct for self-preservation. The framework which housed these qualities seemed of relatively little importance.

Herding and stock dogs

The herding or stock dog is any type of canine that has assisted or still assists man in any given capacity with the rearing, management or farming of his domestic livestock in general. Such dogs did not just happen upon the scene, they were developed from local canidae to fulfil a local need and to cope with the management of a variety of domestic animals, and together with the background and environmental conditions encountered in livestock management this has accounted for the development of the numerous local pastoral types or strains. These fall into roughly three areas:

1. The islands around our coasts, where the earliest traces of habitation, but little early canine history, have been found.
2. Mountains, fells and moorlands, where the greatest variety of herding types are to be found.

3. Downlands, marshes and river meadows as found in Wiltshire, Dorset, Hampshire and Kent, considered since
   Roman times to be sheep country.

Drovers, butchers, warreners, foresters and those occupied
or plying a trade around or within the forests, all owned dogs
which could be said to come closer to pastoral types than the
sporting or hunting types, indeed the latter would have been
frowned upon if not forbidden by the authorities.

Sheepdogs

Although the title of sheepdog is used for several breeds or
types today, the definition of a true sheepdog is one specially
selected by sheep farmers, flockmasters or sheep herdsmen for
its marked instinct or ability to work with sheep. The make and
shape of the dog are of no importance provided it is physically
capable of covering the terrain in which it is expected to work,
but the degree of intelligence in dogs selected for this work is
above average and their memory and understanding know no
bounds.

The true British sheepdogs as we know them today probably
originally emerged from the old forest types. Then during the
Roman occupation, when the wool trade became so important
to the economy, new types were brought in from other parts of
the empire, and as wool continued as one of our main exports
until 1239 sheepdogs also continued to improve. Before the sixteenth century most of the dogs used on sheep in England and
Wales were referred to as sheepdogs, or ramhundts. 'Shepherds' dogs' in the past were body guards or stock guards and
not necessarily herding types, but can in fact be any type of dog
suited to the needs of a shepherd in a given situation or set of
circumstances.

Working sheepdogs

This is a modern title and may seem self-explanatory, but this is not in fact the case; it is a very wide term. So many types of dog today are referred to as working sheepdogs or working collies, and no doubt will continue to be for years to come, but even in the pastoral world things are not always what they seem. Of the thousands of puppies registered as working sheepdogs every year with the International Sheepdog Society, only a small percentage will eventually actually work stock either on farms or at trials. Each year sees an increase in the number of pedigree dogs registered with the Kennel Club in the recognized breeds which come into the pastoral group, and the percentage of these used for the original purpose for which they were designed is almost negligible. On the other hand, a great many dogs kept for herding purposes all over the British Isles are not registered at all.

If a livestock farmer owns a good working dog, it will be of little consequence to him whether it has a pedigree or is registered with any particular club or society, and should he wish to breed with this dog or bitch, the offspring will come into the lower price bracket. However there are those who argue that the modern generation of herding dog owners put beauty before brains, and that this is surely a result of modern living. The genes that carry all the intelligence we associate with the herding breeds are still there, but there is less and less opportunity to stimulate and develop it for its original role, while there are ample opportunities for the competitive-minded to develop the mental and physical attributes of the breed in other directions or to own these dogs simply as companions. However, the herdsman can still continue to breed and work the type of dog which suits him best, but today he also reaps many of the fringe benefits created by the new generation of owners. Television and commercial advertising have created a lucrative market for herding dogs, although this is not by any means always a desirable state of affairs.

When the International Sheepdog Society came into being in 1906 to cater for the needs of shepherds and their dogs, the dogs accepted on their register were, and still are, referred to as working sheepdogs. The Kennel Club also accept working sheepdogs on their register under certain conditions.

The numerous varieties of collie, each bred for a specific purpose, warrant separate definitions, which I have given in the following chapters, but in general terms a collie is a useful all-round farm or stock dog.

Collies

'Collie' is a Gaelic word meaning useful and Gaelic is of course the native language of Ireland as well; the herding dogs there are also of ancient ancestry, a fact that seems to have escaped the notice of early canine historians. Fuller details of the nomenclature can be found in chapter 12. It is interesting that before the Union between England and Scotland, historians only referred to sheepdogs or shepherds' curs; and the Gaelic word 'collie' was never mentioned.

Some say that the collie, or colley in its English spelling, got its name from the breed of sheep it herded. In all the books on sheep or lists of ancient breeds, I have not found any breed listed as 'coly', but 'collie' pronounced by someone with a Scottish accent can sound like 'coaley'. So perhaps this could account for the word referring to the dogs which took charge of the black-faced sheep which abound in Scotland.

One very successful and prosperous Norfolk farmer whom I had asked for information on herding dogs, told me, 'Collies is collies and sheepdogs is sheepdogs, and I owns and needs both.' At the time I thought this a not very helpful definition, but the more I have studied the subject the more I have realized how right he was. Farmers and flockmasters of this calibre make sure they train dogs which show a marked flair or ability to cope with different domestic animals, and this farmer's remark meant he trained a gentler, swifter type of herder to work with his flocks of sheep, while he required a stronger, bolder type to deal with his beef herd. Few dogs are really capable of performing both tasks with equal efficiency, but equally few owners would be prepared to admit it. This gentleman bred and reared high-quality livestock for every category of the livestock market and saw that he had efficient stockmen and stock dogs to achieve his aim.

Flock dogs

Flock dogs are not a distinct breed, but dogs that can work as a team and have sufficient power to manage large flocks of sheep. For generations shepherds and flockmasters have bred and used the same strain of herding dog suited to the stock and the environment on the big sheep runs all over the British Isles, and the requirements are great physical strength and endurance, a strong 'eye' and the ability to work as part of a team and yet use individual initiative when required.

Some of the best-known flock strains of the past were the Sussex and Dorset, the latter being specifically useful in dealing with the headstrong Portland sheep. Dartmoor and Exmoor boasted a separate strain as did Cumberland and Northumberland, and there were several pure strains kept on the private estates in the Shires. In Ireland, too, pure strains could be found; among the best-known were those used in the Wicklow hills. In Scotland flock dogs used on the sheep run of the Border counties are legendary.

In the UK today most of the flock dogs are of the border collie type, but in recent years kelpies and New Zealand huntaways have been imported by flockmasters who felt that breeding of working collies or sheepdogs from sheepdog trial winning stock, the popular lines today for this purpose, did not produce the necessary power for their requirements. Others, however, feel there are still plenty of good powerful dogs working with our large flocks, but as the demand for them is limited, fewer are now bred.

The flock dogs used in Australia and New Zealand today are descended from the root stock of most British herding breeds. They have adapted well to the new environment, climatic conditions and the different methods of animal husbandry encountered in these regions.

Curs or cur-tailed dogs

From time to time throughout history taxes have been imposed on dog owners. It was, however, realized that peasants could not pay these taxes, nor could they live without the help of a dog to guard, keep down vermin or fill the larder. Successive laws therefore allowed exemption from tax for dogs owned by peasants and imposed various forms of restriction on these dogs, such as tail-docking or cur-tailing. In 1796 a new form of tax was introduced with no provision for exemptions, but by that time 'cur' was an accepted title, and many owners of sporting dogs, especially the many varieties of popular spaniel and terrier, had also found some merit in docking their tails, so the practice has remained even to this day.

At one stage docking or cur-tailing of the herdsman's dog or shepherd's dog was the only requirement for exemption, but many 'shepherds' of the higher social scale, particularly the owners of small sporting dogs, also claimed it, and so all dogs with docked tails became known as curs. More details about these exemptions are given in chapter 6.

In Wales the wildfowler's dog which we know today as the Cardigan Corgi (see chapter 7) retained its original role for longer than most breeds, and by so doing seemed to have escaped the wrath of the taxman, but the same breed in other areas which were taking on a more pastoral role, appears to have succumbed to this indignity.

At dog shows held in the latter part of the last century, classes were scheduled for tail-less and short-tailed sheepdogs. It is also interesting that at these shows the classes for females were called cur classes and those for males, dog classes; this was in part to cater for the exhibitors from Scotland where a herding dog was usually referred to as the shepherd's cur if he belonged to a hired herdsman.

In 1878 yet another new tax was imposed on dogs all over the British Isles, though exemption could be claimed for dogs directly involved in the management of livestock, which is still the case today. In 1985 an attempt by a few MPs to abolish the dog tax failed to gain sufficient support in Parliament, but the same question has been brought up again in 1986. Taxes of this nature are difficult to collect at any time, but where exemptions are made it is almost impossible.

For centuries small, snarling terrier types have been kept by Irish farmers and cottagers as guards and vermin hunters and have always been referred to as curs. As a result of their vicious and aggressive nature they are very inbred, indeed it would take a very brave dog, other perhaps than one brought up with them on the farm, to attempt to mate with one of these little horrors. They did however have some use as herders for they kept stock from straying into the fields when being driven to the local fairs or slaughter houses up the narrow boreens or along the roads. Drovers frequently enlisted the help of a few lads armed with stout sticks and a cur at their heels, for they knew every inch of the way to the fairs and all the possible hazards encountered en route, but even this employment of casual labour proved more efficient and economical than owning a trained dog.

Unfortunately, curs being true barkers and biters, cases of attack on human beings and the killing or frightening of stock took up so much time in the local Irish courts, that Parliament declared such dogs to be an abominable nuisance and suggested imposing a special tax on them. The owners who, up to this point, had been very lax about docking in order to claim exemption from the existing laws, then proceeded to have them docked or cur-tailed, claiming they were sheepdogs, and this defeated the new suggestion before it got off the ground. However, in an attempt to make the owners more responsible for the activities of these curs and to save the dogs from further suffering, a special law was passed in Dublin requiring curs to wear a collar to which was attached a piece of wood called a 'clog'. If one of these dogs was found without his clog, the owner was subject to a fine of 10s or fourteen days' imprisonment, always of course providing the owner could be traced; if not, the law had the right to put the dog down.

Stumpy, bob or tail-less stock dogs

Docking has not always been the cause of tail-less or stumpy-tailed dogs. For centuries puppies produced from certain lines in all the varieties of herding dogs have been born tail-less or with only stumps. It is an inherited condition accounted for by the partial or total lack of the coccygeal vertebrae. In most cases these types have turned out to be exceptionally good workers, and are either rough- or half-coated in various colours. In isolated districts where such a gene mutation appears in a good and valuable working strain it is natural that the farmers or flock-masters will want to perpetuate the strain of any such useful dog, whatever type of herding breed it may resemble, and there are still quite a number at work all over the British Isles.

The fashion for continuing to dock old English sheepdogs and corgis when they became show dogs was made for uniformity, because not all are born tail-less or stumpy-tailed, and the lack of a tail is considered expedient on hygienic grounds in the case of the bobtail.

Another line of thought is that the ancestors of the stumpy-tails were brought to England from the Iberian Peninsula

2   A modern border and beardie type of stumpy-tail

3   A short-tailed Irish collie, owned by Mr Kevin Shaughnessy. *Photo*: Sigma Visuals

where a well known breed of tail-less herding dog is to be found, even as far north as the Pyrenees. It seems some of these dogs also reached America in 1800, where for some inexplicable reason, they are called the Australian bob or Australian shepherd. I have seen a number of these dogs in America, and to me they look like a border collie cross, but I understand their method of working and temperament is different.

A most interesting if muddled description of collies and sheepdogs was contained in a letter to the *Livestock Journal* of 15 November 1878 written by a Mr Gordon J. Phillips of Glenlivet under the heading of 'Bobtails'. Reading through it carefully, after sorting out the references to Highland shepherds, cattle, horses and so on, one realizes that he is in fact writing about a pure bobtailed beard, a distinct type or strain of collie found and still found in parts of Scotland, but it is not an English sheepdog.

The Australians have evolved a useful fixed breed of cattle dog known as the stumpie-tail, and although they are unable to pinpoint its origin, they believe its ancestors were brought out by Scottish emigrants. Knowing the usefulness of these dogs even today, and the mass exodus of Scots to Australia in the past, this is a real possibility, but as with the kelpie their history as a recognized breed is the property of the Australians. I have seen them at work in Australia and admired their soundness and stamina.

Many litters born to the early show collies contained tail-less and stumpy-tails as well as normal long-tailed pups, until selective breeding curbed the factor, but it can still occur, if two long-dormant genes are brought together, though this happens very rarely.

In the nineteenth century so many good strains of herding dog had inherited this condition that several appeared in the classes at the early dog shows, but it would seem from reports that the old English sheepdogs were rarely shown in these classes. It was not until 1873 that the first classes for 'Sheep-dogs short-tailed English' were scheduled separately at shows. As the old English sheepdogs became more popular and appeared in increasing numbers at shows, the true stumpy-tailed collies faded out.

Mrs Hill, owner of the well-known Selskars prefix, told me that in the 1940s and 1950s some of her rough-coated show collies occasionally produced a litter with one or two tail-less puppies or even some with natural bobs, as well as those with normal long tails. I have also heard of several other breeders having had this experience of throwbacks in a litter, though they have kept rather quiet about it and had the pups put down. The throwback also appears in sheltie litters and a well-known dog by the name of Tail-less Jack was winning well in shows at the beginning of this century.

Some breeders in Wales and Scotland still keep a pure strain, but not all the pups in the litter will be stumpy-tailed. In Britain such dogs can appear in all the recognized colours and coat textures, but in Australia the recognized colour is blue or blue mottled with tan markings, with a moderately short coat, and pricked up ears.

Beards and shags

These are not breeds or even strains, but a description still used today by local farmers, drovers and market folk to distinguish a rough- or long-coated farm dog from what they term a smooth cur.

The term beard or beardie seemed to apply to any shaggy type north of a line from the Wash across to Chester, and in Wales, whereas in the south a dog with the same texture and length of coat was referred to as a shag. There is still a strain of shaggy farm dog in Hampshire which owners call the blue shag and declare has been known in the district for generations. From the photograph I saw of one of these dogs it looked to me like a cross between a modern beardie and an old-fashioned bobtail.

The original name for the pure breed we know today as the bearded collie, was the beard, the hairy hillman or hairy mould or mouled depending on which part of the country one met him in. The old English sheepdog or bobtail was often referred to by market folk as a shag and I have given more details of these descriptions in the chapters on the respective pure breeds.

Once at a country market in Wiltshire I got into a conversation with a man holding a very shaggy mud-caked dog on a piece of rope, and asked him what breed it was. 'Oh, it's a shag all right,' he replied. I asked him how he knew and he explained that a shag had bushy eyebrows which covered up his mean piggy eyes, while the beard had whiskers and a beard like a sailor! I was certain he was pulling my leg, but I put it down here for what it is worth.

Many other misleading titles like harlequin collie, Welsh blue grey, the tortoiseshell, the marled and mottled refer of course simply to colours not varieties, or are local terms for strains admired and perpetuated by their owners from lines noted for producing these colours.

Keepers' and yard dogs

Keepers' dogs and yard dogs have always been considered as part of the pastoral scene and came under this section at the early dog shows, but as the following extract indicates they defy description.

> From the Grand National Exhibition of Sporting and other dogs held at Crystal Palace in June 1874 comes the following report on the show from a class for 'other dogs'...
>
> Now we come to the class for Yard or Keeper's Night Dogs, crossbred or otherwise. Strange to say only three

came forward. We should certainly have fancied more than three mongrels could have been tempted by a prize of £5. The winner was certainly the ugliest, and looked the most thoroughbred mongrel of the trio – qualifications which we presume were the primary consideration.

Apart from herding duties, pastoral dogs of all shapes, sizes, colours and varieties have always been useful for numerous tasks in and around the farmyards of England and Wales, the hirsils of Scotland and the haggards of Ireland. Others assisted in the loading or unloading bays of goods yards, and the railways kept collies both as guards in the yards and for clearing stray stock from the lines.

Before the days of combine harvesters, stack yards were very important storage areas on the farms, and attracted the unwanted attention of children as well as vermin. The old-fashioned bobtail was said to excel in the role of stack yard guard.

The home farm, always situated some distance from the main house on the larger estates, consisted of separate yards with buildings for stables, piggeries, poultry sheds, implement and cart sheds, to say nothing of the calf rearing pens and wintering stock yards, all of which were in need of protection from thieves, rustlers, vagrants seeking a free night's lodging, or stray animals, wild or domestic.

Foster mothers

A good working dog could occasionally earn his owner some extra money in stud fees, but it was the brood bitch and her additional role as foster mother that frequently helped to supplement the family budget. Long ago few bitches were kept for work unless they proved exceptionally good and these were bred from, either intentionally or otherwise, at every season. If a replacement farm dog was needed, a pup or two was kept and the others were put down, but when the interest in pastoral dogs began to capture the imagination of the public a market was created for these pups.

At times, when the big show or gun dog kennels were faced with orphaned litters, or perhaps a bitch had too many pups or no milk, a foster mother would be needed and a farm bitch with a litter was the answer. Milk substitutes, artificial heating arrangements and feeding bottles are modern inventions, but collies are notably good mothers and will usually adopt any other pup. If fostering proved successful, the kennels occasionally bought the bitch outright and kept her for further fostering at a later date; sometimes she was returned home, but more often she was sold as a pet.

Under the heading of 'yard dogs' advertisements appeared every week in all the farming journals and local papers with requests for foster mothers. The bitch, with or without a pup, would be put on a train and taken charge of by the guard, who would feed her and personally see to her precious cargo, and put both of them on the right train when a change was necessary. A fat tip at either end of the journey ensured this VIP treatment. As I have witnessed for myself, railway staff were often much kinder and more considerate to these bewildered frightened bitches than their owners.

Trial dogs

Dogs competing at sheepdog trials run by the International Sheepdog Society must be registered with the Society, but are not required to conform to a breed standard in this arena, the only other requirement being proven ability to work or control a given number of sheep within the rules and the limits of the course.

In recent years the International Sheep Dog Society and the Kennel Club have agreed to a special working test or trial for border collies which have won prizes in the show ring and I give more details on this test in chapter 19 on the breed.

Sporting dogs competing at field trials held under Kennel Club rules, or those competing in the obedience, working or agility sections, must also be Kennel Club-registered, but in this section the dogs may or may not measure up to the requirements of any breed standard, and crossbreds and non-pedigree dogs may also compete.

Exhibition dogs

An exhibition dog is one which is required to perform a task for which it has been trained, regardless of parentage or registration, except where necessary, with the establishment responsible for its training. Into this category come guide dogs for the blind, hearing dogs for the deaf, mountain rescue dogs and those used for police work. Dogs giving non-competitive demonstrations of work with livestock, or appearing on stage or screen, can also be classed as exhibition dogs.

Show dogs

In all forms of competition some yardstick or guide-lines are necessary for the benefit of breeders and judges when evaluating exhibits, and so breed standards were introduced, but their interpretation is a matter of opinion, and adds spice to the game.

The first requirement of a show dog is that its physical appearance should conform to a pattern or breed standard laid down for the particular breed. A pedigree must be supplied and if the parents are already Kennel Club-registered, the pups can also be registered and become eligible for the showring.

A breed standard is a list of physical qualities intended as a word picture of the ideal specimen of the breed, drawn up by people experienced in the breed, usually breed club members. At first the list of qualities is treated as proposed interim standards for the breed and is reviewed from time to time. If or when no further ratifications are needed, then it is approved by the Kennel Club and becomes the accepted standard of the breed.

Lurchers

Finally we come to a dog which cannot be regarded as a true herder but since medieval times has been part of the pastoral scene and not necessarily always in a sporting capacity. Many a drover or herdsman's family might have gone hungry but for him, especially men and dogs engaged on the long drives, for they were trained as useful providers for the cooking pot.

The lurcher is difficult to define, but was originally the product of a cross between a shepherd's dog and a rough greyhound. From time to time other types or breeds are used, but a lurcher always has a herdsman's dog as one parent. He was so called due to his habit of lurching at anything which moves.

I found the following description of the lurcher in the *Sportsman's Cabinet* and I certainly could not better it, but today he is held in higher regard. It begins:

> 'The cunning you teach me I will execute: and it shall go hard, but I'll better the example' – Shylock.
>
> Though doomed to obscurity by the rusticity and unattracting singularity of his appearance, the lurcher is not without many of those innate merits by which the majority of his contemporaries are more luckily and materially distinguished. Prevented by nature from every chance of dependent society with the great, he calmly resigns himself to the fate so evidently prepared for him, and so truly consonant to the predominant propensities of his disposition. Hence we find him almost invariably in the possession of or in constant association with poachers of the most unprincipled and abandoned description for whose services of nocturnal depredation of various kinds, they seem every way inherently qualified.

4   Hettie, a lurcher/beardie/deerhound cross.
     Photo: E. G. Walsh

5   Tip, a lurcher from a greyhound/collie cross, owned by
     Mr Falkener. *Photo*: E. G. Walsh

4

The Droving Scene

If variety is the spice of life, then it was to be found in abundance in this particular scene of the pastoral pantomime. Droving was usually a family business run by men skilled in the ways of moving livestock, and being a nomadic way of life it also involved many other skills and crafts which helped to

6 Droving scene with sheep, two dogs and a shepherd by
Richard Ansdell, RA. *Photo*: Sotheby's

7   The drover's dog, from William Youatt, *Cattle: their Breeds, Management and Diseases*, 1886

provide a livelihood for whole families. Some of these drovers were also graziers and supplied the local markets.

The long distance droves, sometimes involving thousands of animals, were planned like military operations, and men and horses were specially selected and trained for the task, as were the dogs. As the whole operation could take months the drovers were seldom accompanied by their families on these long drives.

Types of dog particularly suited to working with each type of livestock were kept in packs and were usually quite well cared for, but in any trade there is always a cowboy element and over the years these were the drovers that hit the headlines. Many drovers were casual labour taken on at markets at busy times and these men were often remarkably cruel in their treatment of the stock, which earned the genuine drover a bad reputation; they were probably often the same highwaymen that plundered the drovers on their way to the market or held up the stage coaches.

Certainly it was the effects of the policy of enclosure and the various Enclosure Acts which led to a new increase in the race of vagabonds, gypsies and bandits who poached and looted wherever they went or took their revenge on farmers by burning their stacks and smashing their machinery, and their dogs also played a part in this wanton destruction. Drovers and vagabonds alike travelled the same routes and on occasions they suddenly found their old familiar route, trail or sheep walk blocked off by a new enclosure, and a diversion had to be found. Landowners or the strong arm of the law did not go out of their way to establish whether it was a gypsy or a genuine drover they apprehended for trespassing.

Long distance droves followed cross-country routes in order to feed and water the stock, and up until 1663, when the Turnpike Act was introduced, they used the roads for short distances. The Act required a toll to be paid for every vehicle or animal passing through the turnpike and it then became uneconomical to use the roads. Toll charges may not seem much to us today, but at 5 pence per small animal, $\frac{1}{3}$d per cow or calf, 1d per horse, $\frac{1}{2}$d per ass, $2\frac{1}{2}$-3d for a wagon, it soon mounted up, and caused a lot of delay at the toll gates.

In the last few years a number of enterprising people have set out from various parts of Britain with stock and dogs to rediscover these old sheep walks or cattle trails and have written delightful books recording their adventures which I have listed in the Bibliography. Quite understandably they have been carried away by the beauty of the flora and fauna and unspoilt remoteness of the countryside they travelled, but they do not give much information on the part the dogs played en route, which is our concern here.

The ancestry of these droving or bandogs, goes far back into history, and the family trees of most of our modern pastoral dogs can be traced back to those old droving types. Some of the well-established drovers perpetuated their own pure strain and there are still pockets of these strains to be found on farms today, but to distinguish the individual appearance of any of the varieties would be impossible, for they could be short-, long- or half-coated and of any colour, shape or size. In their method of working some barked, some bit, others herded or hunted, and all were bred from the survival of the fittest. Each variety did however have four distinct characteristics which are, or should be, still noticeable today in the pure breeds which are descended from those droving types or varieties.

First, the bark. Each variety had a very distinctive bark. This was a useful asset to stockmen and drovers, especially at night or in dense woodland, for they could tell from which quarter danger threatened by the particular bark of the dog or dogs in charge of that area.

Second, the feet. Both the shaggy types, the bobtail and the beardie, had or should have had well-arched feet with plenty of filling in the pads to cushion the impact on the hard flint roads, and plenty of hair around the foot and between the pads as added protection, although the shape of the foot differed due to individual gait or movement. Those dogs with harefeet or catfeet and built for speed lacked the extra cushioning in the pads, and the flint roads played havoc with their feet in a very short time. In these dogs the stopper pad and the dew claws took their full share of strain too, and it was not unusual to see dogs arriving at the markets with their feet bleeding and swollen and the stopper pad and dew claws almost falling off.

Gait or movement is the third distinctive characteristic of droving dogs. As a general rule the bobtail worked with the men who accompanied the livestock on foot. He had a slow, ambling or pacing gait, 'gallumping' rather than galloping, and tight, rounded feet which enabled him to keep going without undue stress for longer than his swifter moving brethren.

The lighter beardie type more often accompanied the mounted drovers; his feet were more oval in shape and his gait or movement was an effortless glide at a slow pace and a true greyhound movement at a fast pace. The difference in gait also accounted for the difference in head and neck carriage. A dog moving at a fast pace must have its head thrust forward, but some of the types working mainly with cattle had a higher head carriage.

The fourth characteristic of droving dogs is the coat. All herding dogs have a double coat, a warm fluffy undercoat and a harsher, protective outer coat. On short- or long-haired dogs this acts like an umbrella, and in severe weather can fluff out like the plumage of a bird, trapping the body heat. In the wet the outer coat can be drawn close to the skin to prevent the undercoat from getting wet and to allow the moisture to drip off.

One further complication making it difficult to describe these droving dogs accurately was the practice of shearing, or clipping out the rough- or long-coated types at the same time as the sheep. Unfortunately, unless the shearing was followed up by a greasing process known as salving (the application of a mixture of oils, tar and fats which also acted as an insecticide), the dog could get pneumonia if its coat got very wet. The appearance of a droving dog could vary very considerably according to the time of year or stage of coat growth, and after the shearing treatment many of the driving or guarding dogs like the bobtail, the Welsh grey or the beardie could all look very much alike, though each worked in a very different manner. Even today our dogs look very different when in full coat, out of coat or between coats.

The skills required by drovers and their dogs were often in excess of those required by shepherds or farmers. Drovers going to local marts would work singly with one or two dogs, but for the long-distance droves they formed into bands or companies mounted on local ponies, and used teams or packs of dogs trained to flank, drive, guard or hold. For obvious reasons it was important that each dog should stick to its own task and so the droving dogs were discouraged from hunting or killing. One further type, the hunting dog, was included in the pack, specifically to provide game for the cooking pot; usually a cross between a local hunting breed and a swift collie type from within the team. This was the dog that became known as the lurcher.

The life expectancy of all droving dogs was very short, due to sheer exhaustion, accidents and unfortunately sometimes ill-treatment and neglect, so frequent replacements were necessary. Most of these were picked up, usually partly trained, at the farms or hirsels from where the livestock was collected. Few bitches were kept for work in the past and as the dogs were kept in numbers natural pack instincts took over, together with some harsh treatment for offenders from the stockmen. One hears tales of bitches whelping en route and the whelps being left to die – or in rare cases a drover would pick up one and keep it warm in his pocket and then settle the bitch down with her family at the next farm for the wife to look after until his return. To complete training the replacement would be coupled to a trained dog and therefore very quickly and roughly broken in for whichever task it was needed. Many people believe that modern collies are trained in this way but this is an old wives' tale that is totally incorrect, today's shepherds being so highly skilled in the art of training that such a procedure is unnecessary.

One reads of drovers collecting 300–400 head of cattle from farms in Lincolnshire and flocks of 5,000–6,000 sheep from areas on the east side of the Pennines and bringing them down to the Norwich and London markets. Cattle and horses from Scotland were also brought down in great numbers and I have given more details of this route in the chapter on beardies. Naturally not all the stock arrived at the markets at the same time; they were divided up into manageable flocks or herds and kept by graziers in holding areas or on common grazing land, and in some cases the weaklings were looked after by local families or innkeepers. Drovers often traded in sick or lame animals in lieu of their keep at inns or cottages, or of daily rations for the journey.

On the short drives, a few men and dogs familiar with the routes went ahead to prevent the livestock from straying up farm lanes or into streams, and this is where the barkers and biters were useful as well as within the markets. Dogs which followed the stock were sometimes picked up at farms and were then expected to find their own way home, after herding the animals to a local market, while the shepherd or drover celebrated at the local inn, then hitched a lift home in a farm cart or pony trap.

Depending on the type of stock being moved and the distance to be covered, the drovers sometimes travelled on horseback, but mostly on foot, keeping on the move in daylight and resting up at night, except at full moon, when the stock was restless and the risk of raiders greatest. The men slept rough, at best in barns or haystacks, but the dogs were constantly on duty keeping the flocks and herds together. Rations for each man had to be carried on his back or sometimes in horse-drawn carts. The dogs had to fend for themselves or share in whatever the lurchers caught.

In the very early days only the well-off or well-organized gangs or bands of drovers could afford to travel by the quickest route along the highways, due to the cost of the road tolls. Most travelled by devious cross-country routes or used the old droving tracks. The quickest routes obviously meant less labour and loss of condition but required stronger, better trained and more powerful dogs to push on hungry animals who wanted to stop by the roadside for a much needed midday snack or to linger at the watering places.

Butchers' heelers

In days gone by the local family butcher, and indeed the town butcher catering for a small high-class trade, relied mainly on supplies from small farmers or hired hands who kept a few specialized breeds of livestock. Keeping poultry or a few domestic animals either in the backyard or on common grazing was at times either a perquisite or a part of the wages of hired farm labour.

In the past the profits of the butcher's trade came more often from animal by-products such as hides, hoof, feathers and offal, than from carcase meat, and tanneries and factories were willing to pay good prices for high-quality products if in good condition. This meant not just careful handling in the slaughter houses but careful management of the animals all along the line. High-quality leather, feathers for pillows and livers for pâté were usually produced from livestock kept in small numbers in a restricted area and not subjected to the lacerations or despoiling by undue attention from over-enthusiastic herding dogs.

Butchers' dogs tended to fall into three categories: first were the heelers, useful corgi-like or terrier-types, masters of the game of nip and tuck when persuading reluctant animals to move a little faster to the butchers' holding paddocks or to the slaughter houses. These dogs nipped low to the legs or heels of the animals, thus avoiding any lacerations to the hides. The most famous strain of heelers, to which chapter 8 is devoted, was to be found in Lancashire.

Small numbers of domestic poultry, calves and pigs, when crated, could be brought to the yards by wagon, but at festive times when large numbers were required, heelers, like corgis, were particularly useful for driving the stock or the flocks of geese and turkeys.

The second type of butcher's dog, like the bobtail or larger herders, was used by market porters and others to drive the animals intended for slaughter from the fairs or markets to the abattoir. The heelers were also useful in this respect.

The third type were herding dogs of a slightly more elegant appearance, often smooth-coated. These were used mainly to guard the contents of the butchers' delivery vehicles from thieves – both human and animal – when the butcher's boy was making a delivery. These dogs were trained to run either just behind the vehicle when on the move or between the wheels, and were usually found chained to the trap when the vehicle and pony were stationary.

The choice of a smooth-haired or more elegant and easily kept coated dog also added to the general smartness of the butcher's entry for the trade turn-out at local agricultural shows and other rural events. This form of competition was usually one of the highlights of the show and a great form of advertisement for a firm. Turn-out competitions attracted not only butchers, but dairymen, bakers, brewers and other tradesmen who would all enter their highly polished wagons, vans or carts drawn by gleaming horses or ponies bedecked with ribbons and bows on tails and manes, the drivers and grooms smartly turned out in the livery of the firm or company. The harness and other trappings bore witness to weeks of spit and polish, and even the butcher's van dog, which always accompanied the turn-out, came in for a little of this special treatment, some even wearing brass-studded collars with a brass plate embossed with the firm's name or crest.

Butchers were noted for producing very smart turn-outs and for breeding very fine ponies to pull them. The dogs not only became a recognized part of the turn-out, but started a fashion in carriage dogs, of which the dalmation was the most famous.

All three types of butchers' dog also did double duty as guard dogs in the yards and stables.

Smithfields

These were a specially bred strain of both smooth- and shaggy-coated dogs belonging to a band of drovers licensed and

8   Chloë, a South of England true Smithfield type, owned
by Mrs Dallimore. *Photo*: Mrs Dallimore

employed by the famous fatstock show and market which
existed for a long time on what was then the edge of the metrop-
olis, on an area of level pasture originally known as Smooth
Fields. In 1860 the old market was rebuilt and renamed Smithfield, then a further extension in 1866 soon earned it a very high
reputation as a first-class fatstock show and market.

Fatstock purchased at local markets or direct from farms was
first brought to holding areas around London and then taken
on to the markets. A particularly well-known droving strain
developed for this purpose in East Anglia, and to this day some
shaggy types found in this area are claimed to be the original
Smithfield collies. My own investigations into the history and

evolution of these dogs arose from this claim, about which I had always been somewhat sceptical, believing it to be on a par with the claim that almost any type of hunt terrier was a Jack Russell.

In the history of some Australian breeds the Smithfields are mentioned as being among the ancestors, the impression being given that they were regarded as a pure breed from Scotland, but this is not in fact the case.

To satisfy the new high-class trade of the purveyors of meat and poultry now trading in the new market, stock was not only required to be at the right stage of growth and in prime condition when it left the grazings, but in equally good condition when it arrived at the market. Most of the cattle intended eventually for the market was brought down on the hoof from Scotland and northern England to be finished off or fattened on the pastures of Lincolnshire and East Anglia. The rough-coated old English bobtail was sometimes used on these routes, but he more frequently worked with stock brought in from south of the Thames.

In fact it appears that dogs used by drovers from north and south of the Thames varied considerably in type. The following story told by my husband Tom gives an amusing angle on one version of the origin of the title of these useful canines, which obviously dates back to the days of the early market.

One of Tom's ancestors, Harvey Combe, farmed Cobham Park in Surrey and became High Sheriff of the county in 1831. His father was MP for the City of London from 1776 to 1817 and was elected Lord Mayor of London in 1799, so it was only natural that Harvey also took a great interest in City events. When he learnt that a friend in Scotland, Lord Kintore, intended to send his famous prize-winning ox to the 1831 Smithfield show it was suggested that the beast be sent some time in advance to Cobham Park to regain prime condition after its journey south.

On 6 October the prize ox, its keeper and a shaggy brown dog, the beast's constant stable companion, left Keith Hall to embark in a steamer at Aberdeen bound for the Port of London. In spite of the care of his travelling companions, it was noted on arrival at Cobham Park that the ox had lost some condition on the voyage, and it was decided not to show him until the following year, when he should have reached peak condition.

In the meantime regulations regarding the age of animals entered for the show had been altered and it was found that the beast was now a year too old to compete for any prize. A portrait of the Kintore Ox painted by Cooper, shows him to be a magnificent beast, the result of a cross between an Aberdeen and an improved Short-horn, so this was a serious mortification for Lord Kintore, Harvey Combe and the keeper, though not for the shaggy brown dog.

Only a dairy herd was kept at Cobham Park, so without much work to do in the course of the year, plus the good living conditions in company with his cosseted bovine friend, the dog had turned into something of a roving Romeo. Most of the local working dogs were either smooth-coated black and tan or bobtails, but soon shaggy brown pups with long tails began to appear on farms and in the markets, and tongues wagged and eyes winked! By the time the ox, his keeper and dog had returned to Scotland, the Smithfield venture had become a huge local joke and any local type of dog which had previously been called a beard or a shag was now referred to as a 'Smithfield'. As so often happens, jokes, scandal or gossip repeated over a long period in village stores, local pubs or country markets, are eventually accepted as the truth, and this appears to have been the case regarding the title of the droving dogs from that area, but dogs of this appearance are still found in the district as can be seen from the photograph here of a Smithfield.

The smooth-coated collie, the beardie or the shaggy

stumpy-tailed type, which accompanied the stock from northern areas, also proved useful when it came to driving the fattened stock to the market from the holding areas, like Epping
Forest, and these dogs learned the routes very well. To help
keep condition on the special livestock driven to the Smithfield
market, the cattle were shod like horses to protect their feet on
the punishing flint roads, turkeys wore little leather boots and
flocks of geese were first herded through wet tar and then
through sand, to form a protective covering for their feet, a
process not enjoyed by the dogs. It was said that at one time
there were as many small corgi-like dogs or heelers in Norfolk
persuading their stock to take the 'treatments', as there were in
the western counties.

In the past, so long as the local long-distance drovers' dogs
got on with the job en route, very little attention was paid to the
breeding of an animal suited to the purpose – but with the
expansion of the Smithfield market 'the licensed' drovers, with
an eye to future business, soon found that a selective strain of
dog was to their advantage, and within East Anglia at that time
lay the nucleus for breeding a suitable strain.

In the latter part of the nineteenth century the Scots
'invaded' East Anglia – at least that is how the local people
described the influx; in truth they came by invitation, or to be
more precise by a tempting offer. An agricultural slump caused
by the depression meant that English tenant farmers found they
could no longer afford to cultivate their lands, and a mass
exodus began, leaving many farms derelict in this fertile area. A
far-seeing young man named Joseph Coverdale, who was at the
time agent to Lord Petre on whose 19,000-acre estate were
many such vacant farms, and who knew the reputation of
Scotsmen for being able to make much out of little, had the bril-
liant idea of advertising in the local papers of the Lowlands of
Scotland offering these abandoned farms for occupation at a
'peppercorn' rent, with the proviso that they should be well

farmed and put in good order. Already many of the large estates in England at that time very successfully employed Scotsmen mainly from the Lowlands or Border counties in key positions like gamekeepers, shepherds and farm bailiffs.

Taking advantage of this offer, a number of sheep farmers from over the Border, where conditions were even worse, moved down to East Anglia and settled there with their families, bringing with them some stock and the dogs accustomed to handling it. These hardworking and very experienced stockmen soon made a great success of this scheme. Their stock did well and their collies, which had been bred for generations from the survival of the fittest, and were accustomed to hard work on the hills, made light work of their tasks on the pastures of East Anglia, all of which very much impressed the drovers.

Later on, families from even further north of the Border, who had regularly sold cattle for fattening in East Anglia, also came to settle there. The bearded collie used mainly for cattle and considered to be the old type of droving dog from Scotland which had been brought down by these settlers, together with a few of the border/beardie crosses, proved more reliable; also their method of working was quite unlike that of any of the local types of drovers' dog.

The Scottish farmers and shepherds, through their knowledge of rearing and fattening the stock and their judgement of its 'fitness peak' for market, soon earned a reputation at local and London markets for good stock from the lush East Anglian pastures. At one time there were so many Scottish families on the Norfolk/Suffolk borders that it was nicknamed the 'Lowlands'. George Anderson, now over ninety years old and himself an emigrant from his native glens, gives a wonderful account of just such an adventure in his book *From the Glens to the Lowlands*.

Another elderly Suffolk gentleman of my acquaintance told me his father used local powerful shaggy-looking collies to bring the cattle from the railway yards to the slaughter houses in and around Ipswich, and these dogs were always known as Smithfield collies. The first rail track in East Anglia was opened by the East Union Railways in 1846 and ran between Ipswich and Colchester. Later, in 1849, they opened a branch between Ipswich and Norwich, at a time when this old man's father and grandfather were in business at these markets. The line was later taken over by the Great Eastern Railway which he thought ran a regular cattle-truck service between East Anglia and the London and Home Counties markets. The coming of the railway was the death-knell of the long-distance droving business, but nevertheless for some time the movement of animals on the hoof ·from farms to the loading sheds at the stations and then unloading them at the other end and driving them to the markets continued.

Another theory regarding these dogs was expounded to me by an elderly Norfolk couple. I know this to be a true one for the type of dog they described is still with us today. The old man worked on a farm in his youth, but admitted that he spent much of his spare time poaching or snaring, helped by his father's dogs, which he described as Smithfield lurchers. The parents of both the old man and his wife also worked on the same farm and their fathers owned coursing greyhounds which they crossed with a local farmer's shaggy or bearded-type collies; the union produced rough- and smooth-coated pups in each litter. The smooth-coated were either put down or given away, as it was believed they would take after the greyhounds, and therefore would not be sufficiently obedient for their son's clandestine adventures. The rough-coated pups were kept or sold to drovers or local lads, who no doubt wanted them for the same dubious purpose, because now that most of the livestock travelled by train the need of them for their droving abilities alone had virtually ceased. Anyone who has worked a greyhound will know that they are not the easiest dogs to control or recall once they are on their quarry, and for poaching it is essential that a dog should stop or come back when the handler senses danger, be it from human or natural causes.

Most of the enquiries about these dogs now come from Australia, but if these were the Smithfield types taken to Australia it is not surprising that they proved unpopular out there as herders. One wonders what effect they had on the rabbit population or perhaps even on the kangaroos! I believe a kangaroo hound did exist – and possibly still does – which was said to be a cross between a greyhound and a deerhound! The beardie was a particularly useful hunting and tracking dog in Scotland, and when crossed with a deerhound the offspring were in great demand.

Gypsies, poachers and unscrupulous drovers in East Anglia were quick to take advantage of this trait and started crossing these beardies with greyhounds, the progeny of which later became known as the Norfolk lurcher. Other people I have spoken to said they believed that in East Anglia these beardies were never used for droving but kept purely for herding. However, when crossed with local greyhounds or whippets they made wonderful poaching and hunting dogs.

Research has its lighter moments and here is one which I experienced. Looking through the schedule of the Suffolk Agricultural Society's show a few years ago, I noticed in the sheepdog section a class for stockman's dog, which called for big collie, beardie or Smithfield type, and a silver cup plus £5 was on offer for the class. The class was orginally sponsored by the late Mr W. R. Seward, who I later discovered was head of a local agricultural college and studied herding dogs as a hobby. Like so many people interested in the shepherding world, all his wonderful knowledge went to the grave with him. He must have had some good reasons for sponsoring such a class and stipulating the types of dogs to be exhibited in it, but no one could enlighten me on the matter.

Hoping to get first-hand information from the judge of the class or from anyone else about the Smithfield dog, I entered my big smooth-coated blue merle collie, whose ancestors were all drovers' dogs: he himself was an excellent cattle and yard dog besides being a show champion. Feeling that as it was a stockman's class it would look better if the dog were shown by a man, a friend offered to take him into the ring. There were approximately six entries in the class; leading the parade was what looked like a first cross rough-coated sable show collie, then came two or three border collie types and my own big smooth bringing up the rear.

The entries were lined up in front of the judge in that order. He was obviously out of his depth as to the requirements of the class, so he had a cursory look at each dog, then asked the handlers a few questions. When he came to mine he asked my friend, 'What is it?'. The reply came quick and loud from a man not noted for quiet diplomacy, 'You're the bloody judge, you should know.' The judge went purple in the face, but otherwise kept his composure, and then enquired if he was a good yard dog; my friend snapped, 'Come into the yard one day and you'll find out.' The judge then turned to his steward and requested that the first prize be given to the rough-coated sable, and all other prizes seemed to be withheld; this was a superb gesture in the circumstances and put everyone in their place, but the episode did not help to further my researches greatly.

The Smithfield Fatstock show still held today in London is world famous, but one would be unlikely to see a Smithfield dog there. Their fame was short-lived due to the improved transport facilities for livestock by rail and steamer.

5

Our Island Dogs

From snippets in my heritage collection I felt that apart from the collies of Ireland, the corgi, the kelpie and the sheltie were probably our most ancient breeds, but my efforts to trace their early ancestry were somewhat frustrating, as it turned out I was looking in the wrong areas. Then as the result of a most enlightening discussion with an elderly Swedish woodsman about the similarities of the early trades and occupations of British and Scandinavian country folk, I got the inspiration to look elsewhere to prove my theories.

On one of my visits to Sweden, a great friend wanted me to take back a small present for my husband which she had ordered to be made specially by her uncle, a woodcarver living not far from Västeras, and he had invited us to visit him to see if I thought Tom would like what he had created.

As we parked the car by a clearing in the woods on a sunny but crisp May morning the scene was literally breathtaking. Like thousands of swords the early spring sunlight slashed through the trees to pierce the ice-cold waters of the small lake nearby. In the centre of the clearing stood an enchanting log cabin and in front of it, looking for all the world like the original Gulliver, stood Uncle Lars. As he strode forward to greet us I began to wonder how he could ever have fitted through the cabin doorway, then speaking in perfect English, he bade us welcome and folding himself up like a 5-foot rule he led us inside. His little dog challenged our intrusion and eyed us suspiciously during our entire visit. She was the size of a well-built, well-boned sheltie with a wealth of deep, rich, mahogany-coloured coat, piercing eyes and little ears like arrowheads.

Feeling very ignorant, for I was in fact in Sweden to judge dogs, I asked what breed she was. I was told she was a 'little bear type', very useful for giving warning of danger or trespass, and she was certainly living up to this reputation. My friend, who herself bred shelties and collies, then told me that this type of dog was kept by many Scandinavian country folk, especially in the northern districts, and that they were the true ancestors of the dogs found centuries ago on the Orkney and Shetland Islands. We will return to these a little later.

The cabin was a long and lofty 'open plan' log structure which Uncle Lars had built himself, and all the furniture and fittings likewise. At the far end was a huge wood burning stove surrounded by a variety of cooking utensils, and the whole cabin had the warm and comforting smell of wood smoke and pine. Along the full length of one side was his work bench with all his tools neatly displayed on the wall above. The whole cabin was immaculate. On the opposite side near the stove was what I took to be a wardrobe but it turned out to be his sleeping compartment. The 'mod cons' were housed in a small annexe, basic in design but which would have passed any health inspection. I understand the bathroom was by the lake, sauna style!

My friend had already briefed me about Uncle Lars. (She did not bother to give me his surname, as she said I could not have pronounced it.) I had some idea of the sort of person I was to meet, but the creative, industrious atmosphere of the log cabin was totally unexpected, and I shall never forget the warmth and tranquillity which gave one the feeling that the big bad world outside simply did not exist.

As a child Uncle Lars had helped his father with trapping and wildfowling somewhere up north near the Norwegian border and when his father died he joined the Norwegian fishing fleet. He seemed to have an extensive knowledge of our western coastline which he said came in very useful when he served in fishery protection vessels during the war.

While we sat at the table sipping a thick black liquid he called coffee, he reminisced about his early life with his father and his experience at sea, which I found fascinating. Several times he mentioned bear dogs and sea dogs and somewhere in the back of my mind I knew I had heard these types mentioned before but had dismissed them as figures of speech. When he talked about the fishing industry I became less interested until quite suddenly the gentle giant paused, leant across the table, and with a broad grin said, 'You are an island race, yet you do not live by the harvest of the sea, you let others take it.' Then, running his hands through his shock of white hair he exclaimed, 'You British are an extraordinary people!' To see ourselves as others see us can on different occasions be offensive, flattering or disconcerting, but in this instance the reflection was intended as a compliment and I suddenly became aware that in Scandinavian eyes at least we were seen as an 'extraordinary island race'!

Perhaps it was fortunate that I was not in any position to argue on this point, as he quickly went on to tell me how much easier the fishing and hunting (as he called it) conditions for sea-birds were in the waters and on the islands off our shores than they were in Scandinavia, yet we failed to take full advantage of nature's gifts. I later realized he was referring to the ancient trade in birds' eggs and feathers.

The reminiscences of Uncle Lars and his summing up of our British character, and my meeting with his dog, gave me the inspiration to look outside our islands for the origins of our ancient breeds. I could hardly wait to get home to bury my head in books about life on our offshore islands and the Viking influence.

As we said our adieus he came forward bearing the reason for our visit, a delightful otter carved from a huge node of a local tree, the grain of the wood perfectly following the contours of the body. He said he hoped my husband would like it and then produced a small parcel from his pocket saying 'And this is for you to remember your visit here.' It was a little wooden drinking cup with elk carved around the outside.

Since that memorable visit I have read thousands of pages of island histories and folklore and travelled thousands of miles in an effort to trace the early history of the three breeds which I now feel certain are the oldest in the British Isles, and it has been a fascinating and worthwhile experience. The early history of the corgi, the kelpie and the Shetland sheepdog is so closely linked that to save repetition this extended chapter is intended as one introductory chapter on the evolution of the three breeds.

Corgis

Archaeologists have found the earliest evidence of habitation on our islands around the coastline, which is not surprising as the mainland was dense woodland, swamps or rivers. Stone Age man kept sheep, goats and other domestic animals for sacrifices or other pagan rituals. The main diet of coastal or island dwellers was fish, fowl and eggs, which would also have been the diet of any local wild dogs. Man's talents and expertise for fishing may have been greater than that of land-based animals, but in the pursuit of sea-birds and their eggs, the instincts and specially adapted conformation of the local dogs were superior, and man soon turned these assets to his own advantage.

The Scottish philologist and canine historian George Cupples, who died in 1891, was one of the greatest authorities on the Celtic peoples. He tells us that when migrating bodies went forth in tribal form to seek new abodes, their instinctive desire was for a home as similar as possible to the old one. It had to be suitable for providing subsistence from grazing and shepherding pursuits, as well as those of the hunt and the chase, a desire which unfortunately was not always fulfilled. Mountain chains offered the tribes the most natural migration routes, but on occasions they were halted either by wide, fast-flowing rivers, lack of water, northern cold or southern heat, until turning westwards they finally settled on the coastal strips and islands of Northern Europe. Here, along with the barter or trade in flesh, skins, silks and ornaments, they abandoned the diet of milk and honey and other foods that were the natural products of warmer climes, and were forced to change to trade in fur and feather and a diet which consisted mainly of fish and fowl. This migratory pattern has particular significance when tracing the origin and evolution of the corgi.

The European Cimbi turned midway in their migrations, which brought them up into Jutland, and the Albini came up into Scotland, but both found further progress blocked by oceans, and had to adapt a new set of circumstances and sustenance. During these migrations the rough hill greyhounds which were used for the chase degenerated and became stray remnants or formed hybrid varieties by crossing with wild canidae.

We can only speculate on the type of dog which emerged from this mixture with local wild dogs, but within the last fifteen years the canine researcher Sigurd Skaun has discovered an ancient pure Nordic breed on the island of Voerøy on the southern tip of the Lofoten group. These are corgi-like spitz dogs which have been used for centuries for wildfowling. The inhabitants of Voerøy say they have remained genetically pure

63

9   The Norwegian lundehund or puffin dog, an ancient
    spitz breed believed to be the most likely ancestor of
    the corgi

for thousands of years as no other breed has been introduced on
to the island. The breed is known as the lundehund or puffin
dog, and has unique physical features which equip it to search
out birds from cliffs, rock faces or scree. These dogs are
thought to be directly descended from the primeval dog *canis
ferus*, and are a cynological rarity.

As many Scandinavians have pointed out to me, the great
similarity in the general appearance of our corgis to these northern dogs is too obvious to be overlooked, and one or two of
the unique features of the lundehunds appear from time to time

in our present-day corgis, which I discuss in the chapter on the breed. The limited areas of the British Isles where they were originally found cannot be ignored either.

As with all animals living in isolation, the breeding of the lundehund has been by natural selection from the survival of the fittest, a process with which, in this instance, man has been wise enough not to interfere. However, so much inbreeding meant these dogs had a low resistance to disease, and in 1942, due to war conditions and no vaccines being obtainable, an outbreak of distemper wiped out all but one lundehund bitch on the island. Fortunately a few had previously been taken to the mainland and it was their offspring that revived the breed. When application was first made to the Norwegian Kennel Club for recognition of the lundehund as a pure breed, it was turned down on the grounds that it might be only a species of moo-dog, but it did achieve full recognition as a pure breed in 1943. One would assume that moo was a term used for a general farm or cattle dog in the same way that we use the word cur.

There is also a corgi-like strain known as the senjahund found in the province of Finmark. They were not considered a true breed as both long-legged and short-legged types appeared, and seem to have been a jack-of-all-trades used as bird dogs and herders of cattle, sheep and goats. From their photographs it can be seen that these dogs bear a strong resemblance to the Lancashire heelers.

The products of the sea have contributed a great deal to the Scandinavian economy, and fishing and wildfowling, and not least the oil from the products used for so many purposes were a considerable source of income to those involved in maritime pursuits. For centuries the trade in feathers which were used in so many commercial processes and cottage industries was an important one to all concerned, and as Norse influence spread all over Europe, featherbedding the rich became a profitable business. The pursuit of birds, especially of the puffin and the eider duck, also provided sport, and the tools of the trade were the dogs which nature has so skilfully designed to catch sea-birds.

According to Uncle Lars we lost this market to foreign competition, for in the quest for feathers an annual peaceful Norse invasion came to the islands around our coast, extending as far as the isle of Anglesey, and to many of the smaller islands of the coast of Wales where the Viking or Norse influence was also felt. One presumes they also brought with them their dogs suited to the task. A small trade in feathers and egg collecting had been carried on for centuries, along our western coastline, but there is no reference to any local wildfowlers' dogs until the invention of the sporting gun.

The breeding habitat of these birds are caves in the cliff faces of islands off the western coastline, and from March to August the well-equipped Viking armadas sailed around the northern islands and down the west coast in search of this profitable harvest. The puffin and the eider duck provided the best quality down and feathers, and the eggs and carcases were considered a great delicacy, but had only a limited local market, even when preserved or cured.

Shelties (Shetland Sheepdogs)

Uncle Lars gave me some information on the little bear dogs, but for the information on moo-dogs I am greatly indebted to Lege Per Frey, the President of the Norwegian Collie Club, who sent me English translations of the history of the dogs thought by most researchers to be the ancestors of the original sheltie and kelpie types, before they emerged as pure breeds. I also wish to thank here the many other Scandinavian friends who have provided me with so many details of the Viking connection.

The Viking King Maas owned large sheep and goat farms on

the Lofoten group and kept a number of useful dogs trained both for herding and hunting, among these the lundehund, but all were known then as maastehunds.

In his *Natural History of Norway*, published in 1753, Erik Pontoppidan, one time Bishop of Bergen, gives us the following interesting information:

> The dogs are as elsewhere both large and small and trained partly as moo-dogs, which accompany the cattle up the mountains, round them up and keep watch should the brutes turn up, also partly for hunting, especially the bear, for which small dogs are used, as they cannot grasp them so easily, and which they fear most, for which reason I shall report later in an article about bears.

In this extract brutes mean wolves and I received similar extracts from another source which I mention in the chapter on shelties.

The smaller dogs mentioned by the Bishop as used for hunting bears were the type owned by Uncle Lars. A huge bear would find them difficult to grip, but their noise and heeling tactics were sufficient to give warning of the presence of a bear and delay its passage until the trapper and his big dogs arrived. These bear dogs are said to be the original dogs brought to the Orkney and Shetland Islands by the settlers, but for a very different reason, as I have explained in chapter 14. I must however stress here that the genes pattern of those ancient dogs has been altered by various crosses over the centuries until today there is a 90 per cent transfusion of collie blood in the modern sheltie.

In the ninth century settlers from Norway arrived on our northern islands as a result of a population explosion in that country. An order had been given to 'Go west young man, and seek your fortune'. This had been willingly obeyed and the result was an emphatic conquest of the Orkney, Shetland and

Faroe group of islands, which remained under Norwegian domination for 500 years. Once communities were established on these newly conquered islands the families of many of those seafaring warriors set forth in their magnificent boats, bringing their dogs and other animals with them. The islands remained a Norse settlement until 1468 when James III married the daughter of the King of Norway who handed over the islands to Scotland in lieu of her marriage dowry. In some districts the islanders still consider themselves more Norse than Scottish and many Norse festivals and traditions are observed there to this day.

On some islands seaweed brought on the shore by the gales and exposed at low tide provided additional winter feed for the local breed of sheep, particularly on Ronaldsway, their digestive system being specially adapted to cope with the high mineral content of this food. Early inhabitants built stone walls near the shore-line to keep the sheep off the precious food crops and give them some protection from the stormy blasts. The original wild little hardy and active Shetland sheep looked more like goats and were famous for the wonderfully soft Shetland wool, as were another breed with coarser wool on the Isle of Harris, famous for its tweed.

A small breed of cattle known as the Shetlander existed for centuries on the islands, also one on the Orkneys; the crofters on these islands combined fishing and farming and kept dogs specially trained to herd these shore sheep to higher ground at high tide, and to keep the cattle up on the higher slopes of the mountains away from the crops in the summer months, in the same manner as the Scandinavians used their dogs in their homeland. These dogs were probably descended from the same strains mentioned by the Bishop. All were descended from Norwegian breeds but those of the Inner and Outer Hebrides were much less wild than the Shetlanders.

Kelpies

Research indicates that the larger moo-dogs and others mentioned by the Bishop were used in the management of moose and deer, and were brought by the Viking settlers to the Inner and Outer Hebrides, collectively known as the Western Isles, to help manage the deer and wild local cattle. When the Irish missionaries established monasteries and farms, and brought over the original collies, it was to the islands south of the Hebridean group, so it is doubtful if they figured in the origin of the kelpie, though a dog of similar appearance has existed for a long time in Ross and Cromarty. Farmers who have owned one or two have told me they are of Viking origin, but the moo-dog is the most probable ancestor of the dogs of the Western Isles, and these are farm dogs of similar type to a kelpie in north Norway.

Possibly there were already ancient local herding dogs on these islands perhaps abandoned there by and adopted by the local inhabitants for their own particular situation. On the Western Isles, the power of the feudal chieftains or Lord of the Isle prevented or perhaps diluted any Viking influence as the inhabitants on this group of islands are more Gaelic in character.

Island people cannot gather up their herds and belongings like nomads and move on when local resources are used up or danger threatens; they must either move from the island or preserve and cultivate the resources that are available to them. Successive invaders who have settled on the islands of North Britain have found it more profitable to preserve the local breeds of animals where these existed as they were well adapted to the climate and conditions, than to import others. We cannot be certain if any wild or domesticated dogs originally existed on these islands, but as history reveals from time to time dogs were imported for specific purposes, as were sheep, cattle and deer.

Agricultural history relates how the Kyloe, an ancient Hebridean breed of cattle, the Soay, St Kilda and Hirton sheep, and the red deer all bear witness to preservation, until modern farming methods or economical or political situations interfered, but I can find no reference to any truly local herding dogs. According to MacDonald's *Agriculture in the Highlands*, the name 'kyloe' is a corruption of the Gaelic *kael*, meaning 'highland'. The breed is now found all over the British Isles and is more commonly referred to as Highland cattle. The type of strong dog we now call the kelpie was the dog used to control the big herds and I am of the opinion that the name could be a corruption of the word 'collie' or of *kael*, as many locals believe.

Cattle and deer can exist side by side without poaching each other's grazing, and so can sheep and cattle, but the same is not true of sheep and deer. All three types of livestock are essential to the island economy, so the cultivation of crops and grazing land for each species is as important as the management and segregation of the stock. Part of this island management includes sending the cattle to graze on the smaller Hebridean islands during the summer months, and a very strong, resourceful dog is needed to herd them across the kyles to this new grazing, then back to winter quarters, and also to drive them to the fairs or trysts. Sheep can be transported by boat, as are the cattle from the Shetland group, both to the other islands and to the mainland.

Qualities required of the island dogs of the past were stamina, courage and receptiveness to harsh discipline and living conditions, which can probably only be matched today by the kelpie, but it must be remembered that the corgi and sheltie types of the past were bred for a very different purpose, as indeed they are today, and therefore some physical features have altered.

The management of the cliffs, the shore-line and the quality of the grazing is a challenge to an island farmer, and the products from each have helped him and the economy of the islands for centuries. In the past, the dogs of the island group were each developed to assist in this challenge. The role of their descendants today is very different.

6

Forest Dogges or Collies

The history of many of our modern breeds begins here with the ancient dogs of the forests. Research into their special features and behavioural patterns, particularly of those used by forest graziers, has led me to believe that these dogs may be true

10   Sir Edwin Landseer, RA, *The Forester's Daughter.*
Photo: Sotheby's

ancestors of our modern border collie, a point which I will take up later. My study has been confined mainly to Scotland where I have received great assistance from shepherds, stalkers, foresters and estate owners who have also supplied me with interesting extracts from old game records.

During the Danish occupation of Britain the forest herdsman's dogs were known as ramhundts, shaggy droving types, then from about the thirteenth century they became known as forest dogs in England and Wales. There are no records of how long they have existed in Scotland, but it is generally believed that the foresters used small smooth-coated collie types for the management of the deer, and similar types were also kept by carbonari, men who produced charcoal for industrial purposes. Hounds and terriers also come under the heading of forest dogs, but they do not form part of this study.

In England, the Laws of the Forest were first published in 1598 and then again in 1615 and I quote here canon or article No.32:

> *What dogges a man may keepe in the Forest*
> These little dogges called velteres (small greyhounds) and
> such as are called ram-hundt (a sheep-dogge or Ramhundt;
> a dogge necessary to those who pasture sheep or cattle in
> the Forest) or (al which dogges are to sit in ones lap) may be
> kept in the Forest because in them there is no danger, and
> therefore they shall not bee hoxed or have their knees cut;
> but although they bee lawfull dogges, they must be
> lawfully used and kept: as it doth appear by the next
> Canon . . .

In medieval times large areas of land in Britain were designated crown lands or royal forests, and included dense woodlands, swamps, rivers, arable land and common or heath land, in fact any habitat suitable for producing food to stock the larders of the royal households or for the grazing of domestic animals, and for providing sport and pleasure. Victualling and equipment for the royal households, and for the armies which seemed eternally engaged in a war somewhere, were not over-looked either, as every part of the animal was put to good use.

The system of land tenure has varied throughout the ages and during the early Roman, Saxon and Norman occupations the overlords granted special rights and privileges to the keepers and their dogs employed on their estates, but keepers employed in livestock husbandry came very low on this list, and by 1035 when the conquering Danish King Canute died, the English peasants were deeply confused regarding their rights or privileges. In some districts the authorities main-tained the Saxon laws and customs, while the crown lands which were administered by Canute's henchmen came under Danish law.

At one period peasants who worked or rented property in these crown lands were only permitted to keep small dogs for the destruction of vermin. The requirement determining their size was that it should be possible to pass them through an iron hoop or dog gauge 7 inches in diameter. The laws governing the royal forests were cruel in the extreme where animals were con-cerned and continued so for several centuries. Only noblemen or members of privileged families were allowed to keep the large protective mastiff or mase-thief, so called because 'they maze and fright thieves from their masters'. Hired keepers, shepherds and herdsmen were also permitted their dogs, but all were required to be mutilated in some way to prevent poaching of the royal game.

Mutilation was either by cutting off the toes of the fore-feet, hamstringing or hamling (cutting the muscles in the hams), or making a deep crossways cut on the ball of the foot, but the herdsman's dog was required only to have his tail docked, or cur-tailed, as it was felt this was sufficient to slow him down. Royal hounds or hunting dogs were of course exempt from any form of mutilation. The personal physical dangers of trying to perform these mutilations on vicious powerful dogs made the requirements of the law extremely difficult to administer, and the practice gradually faded out.

It was not too difficult to evade the law, but the penalties for doing so were very severe. Money from these fines was a welcome source of revenue to the crown, so when the laws became unworkable a tax on dogs was introduced, although as we have seen in chapter 3, the shepherd's or herdsman's dog was still exempt if his tail was docked. At this stage in history the large shepherd's dog was still distinct from the sheep-herdsman's cur or ramhund. Evading tax and getting round the law is almost a national pastime, so it needs very little imagination to grasp the fact that many so-called 'shepherds' declared their dogs to be herdsmen's dogs and had only the tail mutilated in order to evade paying tax, while still being able to hunt. Peasants paid rent for the right to graze domestic animals in the royal forests in England, and the forester's dog was a 'jack-of-all-trades', though protecting the stock from poachers and wild animals was their major occupation.

Nowhere have I been able to unearth an accurate description or illustration of a ramhundt of the day, but we can speculate that they were probably a type more akin to a modern rough-coated lurcher. Dr Caius in his *Treatise on Englishe Dogges* described *canis pastoralis* as 'dogges of a course kind, serving many necessary uses and is very necessary and profitable for the avoiding harms and inconveniences which may come to men by means of beasts'. Unfortunately this does not give us any indication of the physical appearance of these dogs.

Reading through some of the ancient laws, charters and historical documents in George Jesse's *History of the British Dog* (1866) was a fascinating exercise and I learned a great deal about the living conditions of rural communities and the high regard in which the animals of the forests were held.

Many of the ancient laws covering grazing rights on common land are still in force today. The Welsh laws or Gwentian code, or the English laws of the forest, did not appertain to Scotland before it was joined to the English crown. The Enclosure Acts responsible for reducing a great deal of common land in England did not apply to Scotland either.

The Vikings made the first significant demands on the forests of north Britain, in the way of material for their long boats. Later came the big felling of the forests to supply the smelting works of industry. The barren spaces studded with tree stumps soon became moorland pasture where deer and cattle grazed happily and by treading in the coarse grasses, sedges and bracken turned it into additional fertilizer, but at a later date when sheep were introduced to this new grazing their light weight did not have the same effect, and resulted in a deterioration of the pasture, particularly as they did not crop the coarser, fast-growing herbage either.

By the sixth century a large portion of Scotland's forests had become common land or commonties. In 1608 the Scottish Parliament passed an Act allowing these commonties to be divided up with the landowners' agreement, and by 1850 most common land in Scotland was split up into privately owned estates and rented out.

While the feudal chieftains of Scotland engaged in fierce encounters to gain more power and possessions, the peasant farmers of north Britain quietly carried on with their business of rearing livestock as they had done for thousands of years, until the demands of industry and then the demands of the taxman changed everything.

Over the centuries felling has continued everywhere, causing the forests to shrink, and hill and meadow farming and grazing to improve. The result was that the herding dogs of the forest dwellers decreased in importance and number, while the need for the pasture dog increased.

In Scotland extensive felling came later and the pastoral scene differed, as did the laws, the wild life in the forests, and the climatic and environmental conditions. Man was more preoccupied with the struggle for survival than the sport of the hunt or chase, but for herding or the pursuit of game, he used the natural instincts of the dog to assist him, just as his forefathers had done. A glance at a map of Scotland will show vast regions marked as forests, but wars and the demands of industry have robbed them of the trees, and much of these areas today is bog, moor or heathland where wild and domestic animals eke out an existence side by side, and where modern shepherds, foresters and landowners hope that by economical measures they can help to maintain the balance of nature, in which the herding dog is still playing his part.

There are areas in the forests of England and Wales where local families still have grazing rights and the shepherds still work their forest dogs, and as local history books reveal, even some of the laws appertaining to grazing rights dating back to the fifteenth century are still in force. The ancestry of the families of the Forest of Dean and the sheep and the dogs of that area are especially interesting. From time immemorial the cottagers and forest workers have been allowed to turn pigs out to graze on the abundance of acorns and beech nuts, and since medieval times this has been known as 'rights of pannage'. The forest dwellers granted these rights were usually miners or men in charge of the huge charcoal-making ovens (a vast coalfield lies beneath the Forest of Dean). These men were known locally as sheep badgers. Holding or handling pens made of hurdles as we know them today were not invented in those days, and sheep were kept together in what was known as a 'haunt', a small clearing or grazing area in the forest near the cottages. When fresh sheep were purchased they were put into this area each night and turned out in the early morning to graze the forest until they had learned their territory, an exercise known as 'haunting'.

The dogs used by these sheep badgers were usually cross-breds similar to types of Welsh hillman. They were excellent guards and used their own initiative to find and return any small bunches of sheep each evening through the thick bracken to the 'haunts' at night. It was not unusual to see these dogs set off, nose to the ground, like hounds scenting along the old sheep tracks, for it was almost impossible to sight the sheep in the high bracken. In sunny weather it was not too difficult to keep sheep together in small flocks as once they had found a shady resting place with good grazing they were more inclined to remain in that area, the dog simply circling the flock to deter predators.

Every owner had a distinctive sheep mark so that if a sheep disappeared from its grazing zone, enquiries were made at work (the pit in this case) and usually brought information regarding its whereabouts. There was a great feeling of brotherhood among these forest families and forms of competition to test the skills of their dogs took place, as they had done elsewhere for hundreds of years, between these miners-cum-sheep-herders or badgers. A sheepdog trial is still held today by these forest folk at Ruardean. Since all but one or two of the mines are now closed, they are no longer mine workers, but many families are still entitled to claim forester's rights.

The natural instinct of most dogs is to hunt in packs, when either great speed or sheer weight of numbers secures the reward. A dog hunting alone will more often use the hypnotic power of its eye to stare out or wear down the resistance of its prey to flight, while stealthily creeping in on its prey until it is close enough to pounce and kill. If a dog is hunting to provide for its young it will probably devour the kill on the spot, and then regurgitate when it returns to the pups, or it may bring back the whole kill – much will depend upon its size and the age and stage of development its litter has reached.

Some dogs, possibly hunting larger animals, will make a

wide circle of the hunting area and wear or drive the sighted victim back towards its home quarters or into a position where it is difficult for it to escape, then leave it to others in the pack to be finished off. This method not only saves having to drag the kill back home, but also lessens the risk of losing part of it to scavengers en route.

The ancient forest dogges, or ramhunds, as they used to be termed, were types selected and trained by the forest shepherds from dogs displaying natural instincts to work silently, flank or cast wide, gather and wear, the very qualities needed in this particular environment. Further selective breeding and regular feeding suppressed the desire to hunt and kill for food. All these qualities are also found in the modern border collie, whose method of working is unique to the breed. Some authorities attribute this to the crossing of collies with gun dogs at the beginning of the last century, when this type of collie was gaining popularity at sheepdog trials.

Forest collies with these qualities had been bred pure for generations, in fact long before the sporting gun or rifle was invented or the gun dog had been evolved. The dog in *The Forester's Daughter* by Landseer is clearly the border collie type, which indicates that a dog of this type must have existed even at that period.

Forest graziers do not need a dog that can drive or chase but one that can cast wide to locate a flock, or herd stray animals, then gather and hold them, and these are the precise qualities or instincts for which the modern 'eye' dog like a border collie is famous. James Hogg was probably the first person to draw the special features of these forest collies to the attention of people outside Scotland in his stories about his father's dogs.

The deerhound, one of our oldest breeds, gives chase in the hope of overtaking its prey by sheer speed, and then either overpowering it by its strength to kill or holding it at bay until the hunter comes to finish it off. As dogs for sport they had few equals but they tended to become bored if required to stand at bay for any length of time, so as individual providers of game for the larder these dogs had their limitations. Working as a team together with forest workers or shepherds' dogs, proved a very much more satisfactory arrangement, but with the invention of the sporting gun or rifle the days of the deerhound were numbered. However, as at first neither the weapons nor the operators were very accurate, many deer were only wounded, and at this stage the forester's useful dog or 'collie' came into its own.

To recover a wounded animal the foresters' collies could be sent out singly or in pairs to make a wide detour of the area, by which time the rest of the herd would have fled in panic, but a wounded deer might not have been able to keep up or if a period of time had elapsed might even be resting in long grass. Once scented or sighted the wide outrun of the collies blocked its escape route, then by gentle but firm wearing tactics they drove it back towards the hunters or kept it at bay. Collies have been known to spend a couple of days in the performance of this task.

7

The Corgi

The principal function today of this delightful little chap, whose early history is outlined in chapter 5, is as an intelligent adaptable companion or show dog. His role as stock dog is minimal, but when performing as such he is usually referred to as a heeler, due to his method of working. His unusual conformation, compared to his longer-legged herding brethren, leaves him no other course of action, when required to do work other than that for which he was probably originally designed, namely, to assist with wildfowling.

Long ago farms around the Welsh coastline were similar to those in Scandinavia and held much the same type of livestock. The supply of sea-birds' eggs and feathers was a lucrative luxury trade, though a more hazardous occupation than farming. The Welsh farmer is a resourceful and adaptable creature and no doubt he reasoned that it was equally profitable to supply that trade from land-based birds and make full use of any of his non-arable land. There was a thriving cottage industry all over Britain in fine feathers and liver for pâté, and in Wales huge flocks of geese and ducks were kept to supply the trade.

Clifford Hubbard, who has probably done more research than anyone else into Welsh dogs, declares that there is evidence that dogs found in the areas of Britain from West Wales through Lancashire and up as far as Strathclyde, are of Viking origin. However, he and other historians of the corgi trace their origin only in the role of herding or stock dogs, whereas Norwegian researchers trace the root stock back to types used in aquatic situations, which may give credibility to the theory that their origin can be traced back to Neolithic times when islander families lived mainly on a diet of fish, sea-birds and their eggs, the soil on the islands being too shallow and poor for extensive crop cultivation.

In his work on pastoral dogs Hubbard says that the early corgis which were taken to America in the eighteenth century were found to be invaluable for herding sheep and cattle, rounding up or hunting stray hogs, squirrels and bears, and retrieving water fowl. They were also capable of throwing a steer by seizing it by its nose. Scandinavian research on these dogs bears out all these qualities, a fact that has added great weight to the theory of Viking origin.

Other historians hold other theories on the true origin of the corgi, and as a canine study their evolution is fascinating. The Scandinavians have no doubt that this type of dog found on our islands is descended from their own ancient local spitz or corgi-like herding dogs and wildfowlers' dogs. It is possible that they come from the group which Caius called *acupatorii* – dogs which hunted birds. It is not clear if by this he meant land-birds or sea-birds, but it is with the latter that we are concerned here. Viking history relates that the corgi's original role was that of a wildfowler's dog, on the cliffs and in the caves around our western coastline, to supply the trade in sea-birds' feathers and eggs. It seems highly improbable that such a lucrative trade was confined solely to overseas hunters, as Uncle Lars suggested (see chapter 5), but I have been unable to uncover any local

history until wildfowling became a sport rather than a livelihood. The invention of the flint-lock sporting gun put paid to
the old-fashioned wildfowlers' methods; the corgi or spitz
types, used to work caves and rock faces, were built and trained
to hunt out live birds; their sight was poor and their pace slow,
so they were not suited to this new form of sport, and were
replaced by 'springing spaniels' as they were called at that time,
trained to retrieve dead or wounded game.

Trigger-happy sportsmen accompanied by their dogs would
invade the more accessible coves in small boats and blast off at
the rock faces. In fact, as a rule, not many birds were killed, but
considerable numbers were wounded or simply fell into the
water from sheer fright. A series of etchings entitled *Puffin
Shooting*, taken from the magnificent paintings of Philip Reinagle, the famous sixteenth-century illustrator, shows spaniels
leaping from the boats to pick up the fallen birds. These etchings are so detailed that I feel sure anyone today knowing the
particular coves, types of gun or the dogs could instantly recog-
nize them.

Through my researches I have only found recordings of
these corgi-like dogs of the British Isles as herders in a land
situation, and as such their history can be traced back no
further than the fifteenth century, yet even today, when latent
genes are brought together, one or other of the unusual anatomical features of this canine family, too obvious to be over-
looked, can appear in a litter. The extraordinary capacity for
closing the auditory meatus of the ear is often noted in modern
corgis, so too is the great flexibility of the neck and the
appearance of double dew claws, which are not deformities but
definite throw-backs to the original form.

Professor David Lowe in *The Breeds of Domestic Animals*
gives a more detailed classification of dogs, which he divides
into four main groups, the fourth being the Indigator group.
This he subdivided into: 1. the true hound; 2. the mute hound;

Herding Dogs

3. the spaniel; 4. the barbet or water dog; 5. the terrier. The
other groups he lists are Lyciscan, in which he includes some
herding dogs, Vertragal and Molassian. This grouping did not
find much favour with the zoologists of the day, but it was infi-
nitely superior and more informative than the one produced by
Rawdon B. Lee in 1894 in which all dogs are classified as belonging to either the sporting or non-sporting group.

Under mute hound Professor Lowe includes lyme hounds
and dogs used by fowlers. These are dogs which work silently,
and the term hound or hund here simply means dog. The true
hound which he mentions is one that 'gives tongue' in the hunt
or chase. It is those in the fourth category which are of interest
to us here, the barbet or water dog which he describes as 'a dog
of Aquatic conditions. His feet are webbed'. As Clifford
Hubbard and one or two Scandinavian authorities have hinted,
these dogs may go back to the Neolithic age, and certainly if
one considers them as island dogs living in isolated conditions
this is a distinct possibility. My own researches, however, only
go back as far as Norse influence on these islands from about
the eighth century. We know that the Viking conquerors
brought their families, and no doubt some of their domestic
animals, to settle on both the offshore islands and the mainland, so it would be only reasonable to suppose that they
carried on with the pursuits of fishing, farming and wildfowling in which they were expert.

A brief description of the special features of the lundehund,
one of the spitz family group from which the Scandinavians
believe our corgi is descended, and which cannot be noted from
a photograph, is of interest when considering corgis as bird
dogs. The first is the ear carriage, which is similar to that of the
corgi, except that the ears can be folded right back so that the
auditory meatus or ear canal can be protected against wind,
sand or moisture. This feature must have been apparent in the
breed when the breed standard of the Cardigan corgi was first

11   A typical Norwegian lundehund head

drawn up. The 1950 standard states under 'Ears': 'and well back so that they can be laid flat along the neck'.

A particularly mobile shoulder joint is another unique feature of the lundehund. This enabled the dog to spread out its fore-legs almost at right angles, a necessary manoeuvre when turning in limited space within the caves. The shape of the front legs of a modern corgi could compensate for any lack of this particular feature. A very flexible neck enabled the head to be bent backwards almost at right angles and was another useful accomplishment when turning in a cave or on a cliff edge. Some of the features also occurred in other wild-fowling/herding types of dog found along the coastline, but as their lines were not kept pure, they faded out. Possibly it was at this stage that the pure strain reached our shores, if indeed a true wild-fowler's dog was not already working here on our cliff faces.

Probably the most interesting feature of the lundehund is the foot. These dogs have six toes on each foot. On the forefeet, five of the toes have three joints and the sixth has two joints, giving the appearance of webbed feet. The extra toes have fully developed bending muscles and extensions. On the hind feet there are two joints on two toes only.

Through lack of use, the webbed foot appearance has disappeared today, and the extra toes appear as double dew claws. These extra toes and joints provided extremely efficient gripping power and balance for scrambling up cliff faces, and together with the flexible shoulder joint gave the dog an unusual gait when running.

Another breed resembling the corgi in appearance is the Swedish västgöta-spitz, to give the correct title, which in Britain we call the vallhund. 'Vall' simply means farm or guard dog and he is in fact mainly a cattle dog from a particular province.

There is a difference of opinion with regard to the place of origin of the vallhund. Uncle Lars was firmly of the opinion that the original dogs brought to Sweden were the corgis which over the centuries the Welsh had turned from bird dogs to cattle dogs. Others believe that the introduction of the vallhund from Sweden helped in the evolution of the corgi as a cattle dog. Some evidence points to the Pembroke corgi and the vallhund sharing the same ancestry, while the same may be true of the Cardigan and the Norwegian dogs, but there is no doubt that interbreeding plays funny tricks with genes, and mutations occur over a period of time. The breed became officially recognized in Sweden in 1943 as the vallhund, but in 1953 the name was changed to västgötaspets.

Let us now take a look at the corgi in his British land-based situation as guardian of the farmyard and collector of domestic fowls. When poultry wandered freely around the farms there was always a risk of a number being taken by foxes or other predators, and a dog was particularly useful in the evening, when the hens had to be gathered into huts or barns for safety.

Huge flocks of geese were reared in Wales as a good source of income to Welsh farmers, but were always a problem to guard. Although they were capable of giving good warning of danger, it did not prevent them from being taken by wild animals like the fox, or by rustlers or vagabonds.

To take a few hens or cockerels to market in crates or boxes was a fairly simple matter, but even one plump goose could be an awkward load, and when it came to a flock ready for the Michaelmas markets or goose fairs then there was no alternative in those days but to drive them there along the road. I have been told that corgis were real masters of this situation. Several could work as a team and once having travelled the route from farm to market place, they seemed to anticipate any deviation the flock might take. These dogs worked fairly silently, otherwise they would have scattered the flocks in all directions, but they were quite capable of removing more than a few tail feathers of any goose that lagged behind or strayed from the appointed path.

Although corgis did take command of cattle in certain situations on farms, it was as market dogs that they excelled. Market drovers and porters had their own teams of small dogs to assist at the receiving and exit yards or bays and with putting the various livestock into the pens (this was also the role of the Lancashire heeler, for which see the following chapter).

Men and young boys armed with sticks prodded and whacked at the unfortunate animals, but a large animal with menacing horns often resented this treatment and reacted in no uncertain manner. A courageous dog that could nip under the rails and give the animal a sharp reminder where least expected often saved the situation, and in the butchers' yards this method of working was of great value.

Most Welsh farmers who have used these dogs for stock work in the past will tell you that local drovers or butchers also used them, but only for very local journeys to the slaughter houses or markets. They say they were never used by the long-distance drovers' gangs who undertook the journeys to the big markets, but when the cattle trade from Ireland was in its heyday, the drovers at the Welsh docks found these dogs invaluable for getting the cattle from the boats and loading them into the railway wagons.

There is no doubt that in their original role as bird dogs the Cardigan and Pembroke corgis of the past were two varieties or types of one breed, but selective breeding from local strains of herding or pastoral dogs, or possibly rivalry among local farmers, resulted in the introduction of two pure strains, and from a study of any known pedigrees two fixed breeds arrived. Even if the corgi fanciers who drew up the original breed standards had a full knowledge of the origin of each variety they could only have based their 'ideal' on what was generally accepted at that particular time as being correct conformation in all departments.

12   A Cardigan corgi, owned by Mr and Mrs Pratt.
Photo: Sally Anne Thompson

13   Lees Honey, a Pembroke corgi, owned by Mrs Pat
Curties. *Photo*: Sally Anne Thompson

Welsh corgis – probably both types – were exhibited at one or two shows after the First World War, but not a great deal of progress was made in the breeds outside farming circles until the formation of the Welsh Corgi Club in 1925, which at first catered only for the interests of the Pembroke owners. A considerable amount of argument took place about the wisdom of limiting the club to one type, and in 1926 a Cardigan Club was formed. Its title was changed several times until eventually it became the Cardigan Welsh Corgi Association.

When one considers the delays and frustration often experienced today when trying to get a native breed recognized by the Kennel Club, and the qualifications required before Challenge Certificates are offered, it can be seen that the corgi fraternity had an easy passage, for recognition came within a year of forming a club, and Challenge Certificates were offered at the Cardiff show in 1928. In 1934 the Kennel Club recognized both varieties as separate breeds, and owners were given a choice as to which breed they wished to have their dogs entered under. This gives an indication of the mixed breeding which had taken place earlier; in several cases the dog's pedigree was unknown.

A bitch called Rose was the first corgi registered at the Kennel Club. Described as a rich red, she was the dam of Phoebe who was in turn the dam of the famous Caleb, an outstanding dog in his day who made all the running at the early shows. Unfortunately he died comparatively young following a minor operation; his son Ch. Bowhit Pepper was his only representative of any note.

At the first few championship shows the two breeds competed against one another. Initially the Pembrokes gained the upper hand, but in 1929 Cardigans won both the dog and bitch CCs; these were Golden Arrow and Nell of Twyn. In 1931 Golden Arrow, by now a champion, repeated his triumph.

Those early days of showing must have been most exciting

and entertaining and I know that a wonderful spirit existed amongst the exhibitors, probably due to the absence within the breed of representatives of any of the big commercial kennels.

Surely the wheel has turned full circle when a descendant of a canine family once owned by a Norwegian king became a royal dog once more. Rozavel Golden Eagle, an impressive name in itself, became the property of George VI in the early 1930s, and one or two corgis have occupied royal residences ever since, with the popularity of the Pembroke soaring as a result.

Many theories have been put forward with regard to the nomenclature, but as I do not speak either Welsh or Norwegian I have nothing further to add on this point. So this would seem an appropriate juncture to halt the story of these delightful little dogs, for I feel its modern history should only be related by someone deeply involved in the breeds. There are several good books for those who wish to know more.

8

Lancashire and Ormskirk Heelers

Opinion varies considerably as to whether these dogs are related to the corgi or not. Some authorities are convinced that this is so, while others believe the differences outweigh the similarities. From my own researches I feel the heeler is most likely a local variety of corgi or spitz dog which has been kept pure for generations within one particular district, in the same way as the Cardigan and the Pembroke corgis. The only real evidence we have of his origin is that of his role of butcher's heeler in Lancashire.

Small farm dogs of the spitz group have been known all over Northern Europe probably for as long as the domestic dog has been with us, but Scandinavians are at pains to point out that although some, like the senjahund, do resemble the wild-fowler's corgi types in appearance, they differ in anatomical construction, as in their method of working. In fact there is not sufficient evidence to claim descent for the heeler from any in this group, which points to the possibility that he is more closely related to the terrier group. There are certainly two distinct varieties. One is the Lancashire terrier type, like the old-fashioned Manchester terrier, and the other the Ormskirk type which carried the white markings of a herding dog.

14 The Norwegian senjahund-nytt, owned by Sofie
Schønheuder

We do know that small dogs from other groups have been
bred in Britain for various purposes since Roman times, mainly
for the destruction of vermin or as scavengers, and they have
not received much consideration. The first book written in
English, the *Boke of St Albans* (1486), mentions separate types
being used for particular purposes and lists fourteen, including
butchers' hounds and teroures (or terriers, derived from the
Latin word *terra*, being dogs that went to ground), but the
most unusual reference is to 'small ladyes popies that bore
away the fleas and dyvers small sawtes'.

It was not of course only genteel 'ladyes' that suffered the
irritation of fleas and other insects, but men and women in
many occupations, especially those working underground. It
is said that miners took little dogs of similar appearance to these
heelers down the tin mines, tucked inside their shirts to provide

93

warmth, or perhaps to draw off the fleas and lice which remained an occupational hazard in those days.

It is really as a butcher's heeler that the Lancashire type was best known, but his terrier character, together with his unobtrusive colouring, also made him a ideal poacher's dog. It was not unknown for a miner owning one of these dogs to earn a few shillings using him as a heeler at the livestock marts on market days, taking him on profitable poaching expeditions on Saturday nights, and then having a bit of fun at the local sport of rat catching on summer evenings, ending up using him as a hot water bottle either at work or in the home when the necessity arose.

It was the export of livestock from Ireland which segregated and popularized this Lancashire strain from other heelers. The expansion in the export of live sheep from Ireland, which started in 1797, was due to the greatly improved livestock accommodation in the cross-channel steamships betwen Dublin and Liverpool. Previously small quantities of wool and a few live sheep had been exported to the port of Bristol, but it was the proximity of the port of Liverpool to the industries of north-west England and to the big meat markets in and around Manchester that recommended Liverpool and first brought these little dogs into prominence as useful herders of stock off the boats to the yards or marts.

Once again it was a rural happening that helped to expand the trade and bring the local dogs into prominence. During the winter of 1829–30, great sheep losses were sustained in England as a result of the rot, a disease of the liver. This caused a shortage of wool and carcase meat and pushed up prices. Dealers and jobbers from the English markets went over to Ireland, where even after freight charges were added, animals could be bought more cheaply. The steamship companies took charge of the loading at the docks in Dublin and every imaginable variety of cur accompanied the drovers employed to assist the sheep from the markets and farms through the dockland into the ships' holds. On arrival at Liverpool docks the bewildered sheep were offloaded into pens and claimed by the various butchers or their agents, who then, accompanied by their heelers, drove the various lots to the holding paddock where they were rested up for a short period, before being taken to Manchester or elsewhere.

Other lots of frightened cattle and ponies were driven on the hoof to local slaughter-yards, sometimes a hair-raising journey through narrow town streets: it was at this stage that these little butchers' dogs took charge of the situation, truly earning their name, nipping the unwilling animals' heels to hurry them along as terriers do. They knew every inch of the way and scurried up side streets in advance of the flock to prevent entry.

Most of this export trade was carried on by the big meat purveyors with permanent premises in the meat markets and was a different type of trade to that normally carried on at livestock markets. The dogs in charge were the property of the company and were normally used only on cattle. It is thought they originally got their name by nipping at the heels while being small enough to avoid the kicks and butts of ferocious cattle. Heelers were also owned by drovers, but theirs is a saga that has passed into history and they are not connected with the Lancashire type.

The family butcher is a man who has always been held in very high regard in the local community and usually came from a well-known local farming family. It was more than likely that his brothers and cousins owned most of the farms or grazing land in the district or held key posts or responsible positions in connection with many of the activities in the surrounding parishes.

One such family from Ormskirk bred a famous strain of heelers, but I have never been able to ascertain their name. It became so popular that almost every farmer in the districts around Preston, Longton and Fylde kept one of the Ormskirk heelers, as they were then called, for general stock work. These were a herding type, slightly higher on the leg than the modern dogs, and most had a degree of the usual white markings of herding dogs.

It was said that a number of gentleman farmers or landowners in the north-west of England who had hitherto owned gun dogs and a variety of hunt terriers now added an Ormskirk heeler to their pack. To own one became something of a status symbol, rather like owning a Parson Jack Russell terrier, no matter what its real ancestry.

Like all terrier types, these dogs were very independent characters and did not show the same faithfulness or devotion to their masters as did most of the herding breeds, the pursuit of their quarry being all-important. This is not surprising since they were not true herding dogs, and due to the appalling treatment they frequently suffered at the hands of man it is small wonder that a sense of loyalty or devotion did not form part of their character. The terrier type was smaller, usually only black and tan, and prick-eared. This seems to be the type on which the modern breed standard is based.

Twenty or thirty years ago almost every farm in the north-west of England had one or two heelers working on cattle, and very useful they were, for they could be depended upon to shift even the most stubborn bullocks. Today there are still quite a number working on farms up in that area. Cattle management is different nowadays, but there will always be a place on farms for these brave little warriors, and today they have also taken on a new role as an exhibition and companion dog.

It is fortunate that so many people became interested in trying to save the breed from extinction, for as with other working breeds, when there is no further use for them as workers they either take on some other role or fade out. Owners of these dogs today say that through selective breeding and kinder treatment they are devoted companions and very accommodating house dogs.

One can only have the greatest admiration for people who strive to get official recognition for our ancient British breeds while they are still only at the endangered species stage, and in this case much of the credit must go to Mrs G. Mackintosh who owned these dogs for many years and put in a lot of work behind the scenes, in an effort to try to preserve the breed and get it officially recognized. In January 1978 together with Mr and Mrs Welch, Miss Jude and Miss Pritt and Mrs D. Rush, a meeting was arranged to form the Lancashire Heeler Club, and in September of that year a proposed breed standard was sent to the Kennel Club. In July 1981 the Club granted recognition to the breed and an interim standard was issued.

The Club held several small shows to help to educate newcomers to the breed and worked hard to encourage other clubs and societies to put on breed classes, but the big deterrent was finding judges with any knowledge of the breed.

The first separate classes for the breed at a Championship show were scheduled at Blackpool in 1982, but there were only five exhibitors and eight dogs entered. The judge was the late Ben Johnson. Best of Breed was won by Mrs Taylor's Feniscowles Princess Tessie: the name given in the catalogue was Tamara of Tapatina, but had to be changed as the Kennel Club did not accept the original. At Crufts in 1983 the eleven-year-old Master A. Kirk won a third prize in a large variety class with his Roseadore Black Beauty at Chesara. He was bred by Mrs D. Rush and is known to his friends as Stillaster Alfie.

Today most of the heelers seen in the show ring seem to be of the terrier type, that is, short on the leg and prick-eared, but occasionally one sees the herding type, higher on the leg and longer in the body, and even with some traces of white markings and dropped ears. The standard is not too emphatic about ear carriage, but it excludes all white markings. It will be

15 Berghof Tansey, a prick-eared Lancashire heeler,
owned by Mr P. Welch

16 Stonebridge Ashley of Sandpits, a Lancashire heeler,
owned by Mrs W. Lewis

interesting to see if in the future, the Ormskirk strain, which was largely the herding type with all the usual white markings, will totally disappear, and with it the alternative title.

9

The Kelpie and the Cattle Dog

The Australians have adopted both these types as their own, and developed them into fixed registered breeds suited to local needs and conditions, while recognizing that at least one line of the ancestry of each came from Scotland and was brought to Australia by some of the early settlers. Many of the older generation of islanders in the Hebridean group, while sympathizing with the Australians for developing such useful dogs, believe that they are native breeds or types that have been on the islands and the near mainland since probably even before the Viking invasions. Over the centuries this group of islands has been invaded by so many different peoples who have each left their mark, that it would be difficult to determine which race had brought the ancestors of either of these types of dog.

The kelpie

Even after an in-depth study of the island dogs, we can only speculate as to whether a kelpie type developed on the islands together with other creatures stranded there when our island mass became separated from Europe, or whether the northern conquerors brought them here. The various colours in which they can appear blend in perfectly with the surroundings in

17   Ch. Jindawarra Jeldi, a Kelpie owned by the Jindawarra
Kennels. *Photo*: Diane Pearce

which they are found, and they lack the usual white markings
so distinctive in herding breeds of later periods.

The story of how I came upon what (for lack of other evidence) is possibly the origin of the kelpie sounds more like
something out of a novel than a history exercise. In the 'bright
young thing' stage of my life I accepted an invitation to one of
those amusing 'who's for tennis' weekend house parties, when
one was brought by a friend and barely knew the name of one's
host or hostess. Rain stopped play, so we all repaired indoors

to entertain ourselves. The tinkling appeal of the gramophone, the girlish giggles, and the delights of the Charleston coming from the games room, could all, I felt, wait until the evening. I decided to spend the daylight hours satisfying my passion for books, and slid quietly into the almost forbidden territory of the huge library.

Magnificent volumes stood like guardsmen behind the gilt grid, and amongst them two small books which aroused my curiosity. One was a beautifully bound little copy of an early edition of *Dogs, their Points and Peculiarities, Whims and Instincts* of which there were several volumes, issued by the *Fancier's Gazette* from contributions by various dog personalities. Turning to the index first, as I always do, I found a reference to Scotch dogs and made brief, almost illegible notes from each in the back pages of my small diary. Returning home I put them into my scrap book and never thought about them again until I embarked on the present study.

In this book was a separate section, for it was more than a chapter, on Animal Intelligence. The information related mostly to large cats and elephants, but the pages on colley dogs also contained the following details about kelpies – the only reference I had come across which mentions such dogs by name.

> On the Orkney Islands I came upon the most intelligent member of the canine race. He is a lanky, ill-tempered fellow with a coat like a bear. The crofter to whom I spoke, while his dog eyed me with suspicion, informed me that these dogs were not only excellent herders but that they instinctively knew the ebb and flow of the tides and strength of the currents. A crofter on the Western Isles to whom he had sold a Kelpie worked him and his descendants for many years to swim cattle across from Kylerhea to the mainland. The old dog knew exactly the

right place and time of day to push the cattle into the water so that during the swim they could be assisted by the flow of the tide enabling them to come ashore at the arranged landing place.

The separate section contained the following odd little snippet of information: 'On the Hebridean Islands are to be found shepherds' dogs with remarkable instincts. They assist the crofters to drive their herds at low tide to the smaller islands for summer grazing and are given the name locally of sea dogs.'

My first opportunity to study these island dogs and personally research their local history came when my husband and I took our first holiday after the war and set out for Scotland to visit relatives and explore the Hebrides if weather permitted. We took the car as far as the Kyle of Lochalsh, and while waiting to drive on to the ferry for the Isle of Skye, a tall, gaunt-looking man with long legs and a straight back strode on board, his neck and head leaned forward as if it had grown that way for continuous sighting of a distant object. Reaching the island shore, as soon as the ramp was down, he launched himself off the ferry, propelled by his cromagh, and must have gained almost a quarter of a mile before our car came off. He strode out like a giant and looked every inch the ancient Highlander in modern dress.

As he appeared to be the only foot passenger on that trip we stopped and offered him a lift. At first he refused, saying his destination would probably take us out of our way, but when he saw our old collie in the back he decided to risk it and introduced himself simply as John. Never was a detour more worthwhile for our mission. It turned out that John was a retired farmer-cum-drover, and part-time school teacher, now living alone in a small croft up a cart track between Struan and Portree. He had been over to the mainland to visit his son and grandchildren. He would not allow us to take him up to his croft, saying it was the only dwelling for miles, with a rough approach, but invited us to visit him later if we wished while we were on the island.

He seemed such an interesting and knowledgeable personality that we did plan a visit a few days later and bumped our way to his croft along the rutted cart track. It was one of those memorably fine days that it is sometimes the visitor's good fortune to enjoy on Skye. We sat in the sun on a bench outside the croft armed with mugs of tea, while a few hens scratched the ground at our feet. The presence of our dog provided the perfect opportunity to continue the conversation regarding local dogs we had touched upon a few days earlier. John fondled our dog's head and ears while he told us he felt it was unfair to keep a dog these days as he had no work for one now. As he frequently went to visit his son he could not take it with him and there was no one near to look after it, so the hens had to fend for themselves.

While recalling the dogs he had owned, John referred to them as kelpies not collies. Naturally this intrigued me, so by a process of question and answer I pieced together the following information which could well be the true origin of the kelpie. It is certainly more convincing than any connection with a cross between a fox and a collie, as has sometimes been suggested. There is a Scandinavian theory that the ancestors of these dogs were the original bear dogs of the forest and to be found all over northern Europe at the time our land masses were united after the Ice Age. There is more about this in the chapter on shelties. If the theory is correct then there may be some foundation in the fox connection, but this can only be a matter of speculation now.

According to John this type of short-haired herding dog had been on the islands since time immemorial. For intelligence and stamina he said they were unbeatable, the best in the world – they seemed to grow out of the soil. They were totally devoted to the family, coming in and out of the crofts as they pleased by day, but took up a well-concealed guarding position outside at night and would swim out to greet the fishing boats returning to shore.

He described them as being big enough to come up to his knee, but lightly built with a black or grizzly brown coat of the same texture as that of a bear. He was of the opinion that the term 'bare-skinned dogs' originally meant just that – 'bear-skinned' – not as the English use the description for a smooth-coated dog. He said the coat was harsh to the touch and totally water-resistant, and that these dogs had exceptionally strong, hard feet.

A pure strain of all-black or black-and-tan herding dog existed for centuries in the kingdoms of northern Scotland we now call Ross, Cromarty and Sutherland. Occasionally a brown or chocolate one was found, due to the particular genetic colour inheritance factor. John said they were particularly suited to herding the small breed of Sutherland cattle and those from Caithness which were later crossed with those from Argyle and Skye, but not being a sheep man, his particular interest in these dogs lay with cattle.

In an Australian book I found a photograph of Coil stating that he was an outstanding winner in early sheepdog trials (presumably at the end of the nineteenth century). From the illustration it seems that his appearance is remarkably like the old original dogs of the Orkney and Shetland groups.

Although they had never been regarded as a breed, John told us there were still some strains of these dogs to be found working sheep and cattle for crofters in remote highland and island areas. He thought that at one time the corgi and these kelpies or kyle dogs were interbred as both had the same type of head and very similar behavioural patterns and instincts, but it was mostly as cattle dogs that he came into contact with them, especially their use in driving the cattle across the kyles to summer grazing on the smaller islands. He thought that the name kelpie was probably a corruption or an abbreviation of the title 'kyle collie'.

With regard to this, it is interesting to note that the breed standard of the kelpie, as laid down by the Australian Kennel Control Council, states that the head is similar to that of a corgi, the coat weather-resistant and that good strong feet with a spring of pastern are essential, which leads one to suppose that these features must have been present in the original dogs brought out by the settlers. Certainly our friend John had never heard of a breed standard.

Island people are very superstitious, especially the fisher folk, and an amusing, more romantic version of the kelpie was given to us by one or two of the older generation of islanders. For their version we must go back several thousand years to the time when the inhabitants of the islands worshipped and made sacrifices to the gods of sun and water, and mythology played a large part in their lives. According to these old folk, kelpie was the Gaelic name for a water sprite in the form of a young, spirited animal that frightened off anything approaching a water hole (on some of the islands of the Hebridean group there is more water in the form of lochs than there is land mass). One old lady told me with a wicked grin that they used to send the 'spirit' over to the mainland to frighten away the warriors collecting at the kyles or crossing points.

Since the breed was no longer considered British this was as far as I felt necessary to try to trace its origin, but a most convincing account of the possible origin of the Australian kelpie was sent to me by Chris Chapman of Engadine who has done an enormous amount of research on the subject. According to her findings, prior to 1870 a grazier from Worrock station, Victoria, by the name of George Robertson, imported a pair of black and tan collies from Sutherland and had a litter from them. One of the bitch pups went to a Mr Gleeson, believed to be an Irishman, on the adjoining station of Dunrobin, and he gave the bitch the Gaelic name of Kelpie. She proved to be an exceptionally good worker and he took her with him when he moved to North Bolero in New South Wales where he met a Mr Tully who owned an all-black dog called Moss. Later Gleeson acquired Moss and mated Kelpie to him. The pups from the resulting litter turned out to be such good workers that the kelpie strain became quite famous.

A branch of the Rutherford family from Sutherland having emigrated to Yarrawanga many years earlier had imported a pair from their Scottish home and Moss was a descendant of that original brace. The Rutherford family in Scotland later sent out another brace to a Mr Elliot and Mr Allan of Geraldra on the Lachlan river near Forbes.

In his book *Australian Barkers and Biters* Robert Kalaski gives this pair the credit for originating the breed in Australia, but according to the records in the archives of the Mitchell Library the credit would appear to go to the brace previously imported by the Rutherfords. His book is now out of print and it is very difficult to obtain old copies, but an interesting extract regarding these imports appears below.

THE KELPIE

His Ancestry and Progeny

To look at the Kelpie you would think he is a cross between the Smooth collie and the Dingo; but he is not, though most bushmen will fight you if you say so. Nearly all have the idea that he sprang from a cross of the Dingo and the Collie made by an old shepherd at Humbug Creek, near Condobolin. But this is not the case. Men from the border of Scotland and England whom I have met out here say that he comes from a cross of Fox and Black Smooth Collie made by a gipsy for a poaching dog a hundred years ago. The true story of the Kelpie's origin is best told by the man who knew it best, in his own words – Phil Mylecharane, a connection of mine, who used to be with Mort's, and who judged the first Sheep-dog trial ever held in Australia, where the original bitch – Kelpie's Pup – won and made the name which has been made common to all her descendants. (About this time shepherding, with its small mobs and rough-haired Collies to handle them, had gone out; as land was getting dear, fencing had come in, and with it big mobs and the need of a suitable dog to work them.)

In 1870 I went out to Mr Allan, of Geraldra Station, to buy flock rams for Mort and Company. When I got there, Mr Allan told me that the rams were out in the paddock, but he would soon get them in for me. So saying, he opened the yard-gate, whistled up two smooth, prick-eared black-and-tan dogs, a male and a female, and sent them out into the paddock.

In a very short time they were back with the rams, and put them into the yard. I never saw dogs work sheep before as these two did, and, noticing that the bitch had pups, made up my mind I must have one. So after I bought the rams (I took a big lot of them) I said to Mr Allan, 'Where did you get these dogs?'

His answer was that he had just imported them from Scotland, from a wonderful working strain there. The dog's name was Brutus and the slut's Jenny.

'Well,' I said, 'what about a pup for me?' He told me I could have one, but there was only one left and he thought I wouldn't like its color. We went round to see the pups, and he pointed mine out – a little red-colored one, exactly like a little Dingo; the rest were black and tan.

'Oh,' I said, 'I won't have him; he's a Dingo.' Mr Allan assured me that this was impossible, as the pups were sired on board and every care taken. He advised me to take the pup and he would write home to the breeders and see about it. I took his advice and the pup. The latter turned out a splendid worker. After having him for two years, he was stolen from me down at Goolagong, near Forbes.

The next time I saw Mr Allan he told me that the breeders of Brutus and Jenny had written back to say that in nearly every litter they got a similar pup to mine and that they were great workers. So that disposed of the Dingo theory.

About this time, or a little later, a Mr Gleeson came to the Lachlan with a prick-eared, smooth-haired black-and-tan bitch he called Kelpie. He mated her to a son of Brutus and Jenny called Caesar, and he gave one of the pups, a black-and-tan bitch, to Mr C. B. W. King, then managing Wollongough Station, Humbug Creek, near Condobolin. Mr King called her Kelpie, after her mother, and she won at the Forbes Trial and made a name for herself. The pups were called Kelpie's pups, and so the name spread.

One of her daughters, called Sally, was mated to Moss, a black dog from Brutus and Jenny's strain, and one of the pups, called Barb after the well-known Cup-winner, was sold by a half-caste (Davis) who owned him to Mr Edols, of Burrawang. Barb's pups made a name for themselves just as Kelpie's had done, and were called 'Barbs'. Both the Kelpie and Barb, therefore, were started by Brutus and Jenny's Caesar and Gleeson's bitch Kelpie.

So that is how the kelpie, as a breed, originated. I have

never been able to find out the pedigree of Gleeson's
kelpie, though I have spent a great deal of money and time
on it. She must have been a wonderfully potent female and
was lucky in being mated with such a good strain as
Caesar's. Their progeny would keep improving of course,
if carefully bred, as they became acclimatized, and their
descendants, improving all the time, are the kelpies of
today.

The cattle dog

John was firmly of the opinion that the modern Australian
breeds like the cattle dog and the kelpie stem from the same
spitz ancestry which had been in existence for thousands of
years and even possibly still existed as recently as a few centuries ago on these islands. He gave me a number of reasons for
putting forward this theory, his chief one being the colour inheritance factor. All the early island dogs were merle-coloured,
which blended perfectly with the environment in which they
worked. He believed that any solid-coloured dogs which
appeared in these types were those introduced to the mainland
to work in the forests helping with the management of the deer
and cattle.

He had bred and used this type of cattle dog most of his life
and said it would be almost impossible for anyone who had not
worked a dog of this nature to understand their true value. If a
sheep or a cow was perched on a cliff top or a lower edge these
dogs were capable of quietly approaching or outflanking the
animal and turning it or backing it away from danger, and then
moving in to give it a quick nip to send it on its way. The dog's
unobtrusive colouring did not alarm the animal.

John was fully convinced that the original wild-fowling
instincts were still alive in these dogs which he had found so
useful for dealing with cattle, but he believed modern breeders
were more concerned with the popular fashion for breeding to

18 A group of Australian cattle dogs, owned by Mr John
Holmes. *Photo*: Sally Anne Thompson

type. In nature, breeding from the survival of the fittest under
local conditions would keep a type or breed pure if not interfered with by man, while still retaining its natural instincts.

I shall always regret that at the time I did not fully appreciate
the importance of these island dogs in our herding history, for
it may never again be my good fortune to meet such a fountain
of knowledge on this particular subject. John and I had some
discussion on the question of how the white points became a
trade mark of some of our herding dogs. He was of the opinion

19 The Australian cattle dog at work, owned by Mr John
Holmes. *Photo*: Sally Anne Thompson

that the foresters could see a solid-coloured dog better in the forests but that those displaying some white points could be seen more easily when on the move. In the short daylight hours a great deal of stock work had to be done by lantern light and it was surprising how the white feet, the white tip to the tail and the white on the head and chest showed up in the light of a lantern, enabling the herdsman to follow his dog, his scenting ability guiding him.

10

The Scotch or Highland Collie

The noble sight of a Scottish shepherd and his dog has captured the imagination of artists and poets for centuries, and canine historians have claimed that the ancestors of many of our

20 Richard Ansdell, RA, *Highland Collie* (1871).
Photo: Sotheby's

modern pastoral breeds originated in Scotland. The rough- and smooth-coated show collies are frequently referred to as Scotch collies, as are the beardies; I dispute the assumption and give my reasons in the chapters on the respective breeds. If this were so, why is there no officially recognized fixed pure breed known as Scotch or Highland collie registered with the Kennel Club? Yet on the Continent of Europe the show collie is known as *berger écosse* (Scotch sheepdog).

Ask anyone either at home or abroad what the Scotch collie means to them and the answer would probably be 'The world's most famous sheepdog'. But ask them to describe the dog and I hazard a guess that no two people would give the same picture. One is left wondering exactly how one could describe a true Scotch collie, for the herding dogs of Scotland as elsewhere differed greatly from region to region. As I have explained in the chapter on Irish collies, the appellation 'collie' (or 'colley' as it it is spelt in old English) is old country Gaelic meaning anything useful, thus a collie dog was the useful farm or shepherd's dog of Scotland and Ireland. After the Union between England and Scotland some useful herding dogs became known as collies south of the Border too, being mostly descended from Scottish dogs.

Canine historians of the past frequently refer to the herding dogs of Scotland as collies, but in other parts of the British Isles they became sheepdogs, drovers' dogs, farm dogs or curs. Arthur Croxton Smith was an authority on working dogs and his *British Dogs at Work* (London 1906) was a valuable contribution to herding literature. He was chairman of the Kennel Club from 1937 to 1948 and also chairman of the Guide Dogs for the Blind during that period. He observed in one of his articles in *The Field* that most early references to sheepdogs refer to English dogs, and that there appears to be a dearth of records for the dogs of the lands north of the Border. He went on to say, 'History is blank about the Scottish collies at that period – possibly there were none, for the Scots were long behind in developing their natural resources. When they did take to pastoral pursuits they had to enlist the aid of dogs for work in hilly country, enclosures not being as common as they were in England.'

The time he was referring to was the late sixteenth century, when much of Scotland was still covered by dense forests. The enclosure system would have been impossible to implement in the majority of the regions, but animal husbandry has been an important way of life and source of income to the crofters for centuries. We know too that herding dogs, including the collies brought over from Ireland, have worked on the moors, mountains and in the forests of North Britain, as it used to be called, for some considerable time. Each region bred its own pure strain suited to the local conditions. James Dalgliesh in his chapter on collies in Leighton's *New Book of the Dog* (1907), refers to the bearded collie as the Scottish or Highland collie, but other authorities would not go along with this.

In part, I agree with Mr Croxton-Smith's statement, for most of the early references to herding dogs of Scotland were just stories of the sagacity and faithfulness of some particular dog. However, the earliest 'authentic' records and pedigrees of these dogs that I could trace have been supplied to me by the Royal Archives at Windsor and concern the pedigree of dogs belonging to Queen Victoria. It appears that from 1844 to 1866 all these dogs were described as 'Highland sheepdogs', but from then onwards they were described as Scotch collies.

In *The Dog* (1849 and reprinted in 1879), William Youatt devotes a chapter to the Scotch sheepdog. In content it mainly quotes from the writings of James Hogg, but there is an illustration reproduced here which one presumes portrays the make and shape of a Scotch collie of the day.

In a chapter on colleys Edward Jesse (1896) gives some rather confusing details about a Scotch colley saving the life of a

21 A Scottish sheepdog, from William Youatt, *The Dog*, 1879

child in the Grampians, and George R. Jesse (1866) only mentions them with regard to their worth in ancient laws and charters. Other writers have lumped together all the herding strains or breeds of Scotland under the title Scotch collie or colley. There is a little more information on this understanding of a Scotch colley in the chapter on the Rough Show collie. It is also worth noting that the spelling of the collie in both texts is the English version.

My own attempts at research by personal contacts were not always rewarding. In one or two instances I was regarded as a busybody, while others treated me to the story of their lives, or the case history of every dog they had owned, together with endless but fascinating reminiscences, all of which were enthralling but not exactly helpful to my quest. The dignity of Scottish country folk, their high regard for traditions and their deep respect for religion in the face of modern living conditions, make one feel very humble and grateful for the continuance of their way of life – long may it remain so.

Most of the people to whom I spoke referred me to the writings of James Hogg, Robert Burns, Robert Louis Stevenson, Sir Walter Scott and many others. I was also treated to some delightful and nostalgic tales about life and working conditions on the Lammermuir, Pentland or Lowther Hills, to say nothing of countless episodes which took place on the Cheviots and in the Border counties. I have had to resort to political and social history to give a picture of how Scottish herding dogs came on the modern scene.

It is interesting that for centuries a dog known only as the shepherd's dog or sheepdog and of similar type and appearance has worked on farms and sheep runs all over the British Isles, but this type has not inspired poets and artists like those dogs of Scotland. I suspect that the glamour of the kilt and the ruggedness of the scenery may have had their part to play in this.

As hinted at by Croxton-Smith, farming in general in Scotland did not contribute to the economy to any great extent while the feuding and fighting among the clans in the Scottish glens was in progress, so the farms and farming communities became more and more neglected and the land impoverished. Because rents were low, if in existence, the Highland landowners felt they were insufficiently reimbursed. This was especially true after the Union with the English crown when they were required to pay higher taxes; thus a means had to be found whereby the land could be made profitable.

Backed by political economists, the decision was taken to stock the Highland region with sheep, to bring in extra revenue, a move which had proved highly profitable in other regions. Parcels of grazing land were offered for low rents, but at prices still beyond the purses of the local crofters. The scheme attracted sheep farmers mostly from the Border counties who stocked the grazing with black-faced and Cheviot sheep and then returned to their farms, in some cases employing a few local crofters to look after the flock. From the start the scheme proved unsatisfactory, for the pasture was more suited to deer and cattle. Sheep cropped the herbage on the lower slopes so close that it did not have time to recover before bracken – toxic to sheep if eaten in any quantity – took over. Dipping was unknown in the region in those days, so the maggots hatched from the eggs of the blow-fly or blue-bottle, which thrive in bracken, plus starvation in the winter months, took heavy toll of the sheep. Many losses were also sustained through accidents as the local hill and forest dogs, more used to working with deer and cattle, killed many lambs and often pushed the flocks too fast so that they fell over the steep edges. The sheep that did survive and became acclimatized, became known as forest breeds.

Even with the balance of nature upset and the crofting life disrupted, the stout-hearted Highlander still continued to eke out an existence from deer and cattle. In his poem 'The Last Deer of Beinn Doran', written about 1800, John Hay Allen recounts how this move by the chieftains a century earlier, drove the superior deer of Glen Urcha away to the mountains of Beinn Doran through lack of grazing and poaching, until the very fine deer in that region became extinct.

When extra revenue is needed governments tend to go overboard on agricultural schemes, and in the nineteenth century Parliament hit upon yet another such scheme. This time it was found necessary to introduce a new race of men to accomplish the task of rehabilitating the area. The scheme caused a great deal of hardship and bitterness among the already impoverished peasants, and these 'foreigners' met fierce hostility from the locals. Their sheep were rounded up and driven over cliff edges to die in deep gullies or drown in the lochs, while some were driven into neighbouring counties to be dealt with by other angry mobs.

The strong arm of the law was then applied, and the Highlanders were evicted from their miserable farms and shealings, an operation known as the 'Highland Clearances'. Most of the 'foreigners' who took over the region were shepherding families from the southern Uplands, the Lowlands or the Border counties. Many single men of evicted families sought employment in England, others went overseas and took their dogs with them, while a number of families took refuge in a settlement at Bettyhill founded for them by Elizabeth, Marchioness of Stafford.

Just as one consequence of the Plague was to bring attention to the English shepherds and their dogs, so the Highland Clearances later brought the Scottish shepherd and his collies into prominence, a position they have held ever since. In fact they are probably the best ambassadors Scotland has ever produced.

Almost a century later when the new railway system and improved accommodation on the steam packet shipping lines made travelling easier, the sheer beauty of the scenery and the excellent sporting facilities attracted wealthy families for fishing, stalking and sailing. Owners of large estates all over Britain, while visiting Scotland, were so impressed by the intelligence of the local herding dogs and the close relationship between them and the shepherds, but so appalled by the impoverished conditions, that they persuaded many shepherds to take up employment on English estates and move with their families to a better environment and better living standards. Those hardworking families that did move made a great success of the venture, to such and extent that if an estate employed a Scottish shepherd and his collies it was considered particularly wise management. By the middle of the last century owning a collie became almost a status symbol and was particularly fashionable with the ladies.

This was also the period when, due to royal patronage at Balmoral, a fashionable interest was being taken in the Scottish pastoral scene. English and overseas visitors came to Scotland for the sport, bringing their own sporting dogs, as was the custom. There were no rabies restrictions in those days. The Brittany spaniel was a popular dog with French sportsmen, but its intelligence and trainability did not match that of the local collies, and many owners had their bitches mated to local collies to improve the performance of gun dogs in general, both British and Continental. The result did much for the gun dogs but little for the collies, and the cross was most noticeable in the appearance of the offspring of the Scottish collies of a later period, compared to the English sheepdogs. This was particularly evident in head properties – for example, a lower ear carriage and heavier ears were introduced. The colours of the original black and tan characteristic of the true Scottish collie were also altered.

The popularity and novelty of dog shows on the English scene aroused the curiosity of wealthy Scotsmen, and brawny men sporting the kilt and the tam o'shanter travelled with their dogs to the early shows in order to reap the benefits of this new, lucrative market. The new, wealthy fanciers of the collie, including Americans with fat cheque books, and the big breeding or show kennels in England, were all eager to buy these Scottish dogs. The black, tan and white so-called Highland collies fetched the highest prices. Collies in other colours which were considered as Lowland were not so fashionable just then.

The very first entry in the Kennel Club stud book under colleys and sheepdogs was Glen, a black, white and tan dog born in 1866 belonging to a Mr Field and described as an

Argyllshire sheepdog. In fact all manner of local names were given to the entries at the shows. One presumes the exhibitors classed these dogs according to the district from which they came. In one report I read that on no account should the all-black pure Ross-shire sheepdog be considered for high honours, but no reason was given for this. The black, tan and blue merle or marbled were declared to be the only true representatives from north of the Border, which is all rather confusing. More details of the Ross-shire dogs are given in the chapter on kelpies and may have been legitimate reason for this argument.

The judges at those early shows were mainly gentlemen whose knowledge of the gun dog was superior to that of the pastoral breeds, so frequently it was a case of the wrong end of the lead being judged. Fights between both men and dogs were commonplace and many unpleasant incidents occurred which incensed the professional shepherds to such a degree that avoidance of the whole show scene in general became an obsession, which has continued through generations of farming families to this day.

Performance, not looks, is what shepherds and flockmasters required of their dogs, so they left their good-looking aristocrats to the show fraternity and returned to their native hills and hirsels to continue breeding working dogs. At the same time, the growing popularity of sheepdog trials produced yet another Scottish collie. It was not size or colour, but the method of working, which captured the imagination of the public, but I tell the story in chapter 19, for this dog became known as the border collie, although his origin may have been among early forest collies, found all over the British Isles.

As 'like breeds like', it follows that certain similar physical features became constant in the dogs found working in each region. The special attributes for which the Upland, Lowland and Highland collies became famous have been carefully preserved through selective breeding. Several of our modern hill and fell 'all-purpose' versatile types are descended from the mountain and moorland collies of Scotland, so too are many of the ancient pure strains used by the shepherds and flockmasters on the sheep runs of our Border counties, and those taken overseas by settlers, be they registered or unregistered, titled or untitled.

The study of Scottish dogs necessitated digging deep into social and rural history of the past. During the process it became even clearer to me that poets and painters have been largely responsible for romanticizing and popularizing the Scottish scene, and subsequent royal connections have made it fashionable. Journalists and dog breeders were among those who jumped on this bandwagon. Scottish terrier breeds began to oust the popular English terriers, and almost every variety of herding dog was soon claimed to be of Scottish origin. Researches do not substantiate this claim. But today it might be difficult or even unpopular to try to convince the owners of those glamorous show collies that their original ancestors came from the bogs of Ireland and not from the hills of Scotland.

11

The Welsh Sheepdog/Collie

For many years we owned a succession of dogs referred to as Welsh collies. They had certainly been bred in Wales and we travelled to remote farms in the Principality to collect the pups. Imagine, then, my surprise when digging deep into the history of our pastoral breeds, to discover that there is no such breed recognized or registered under either title with the International Sheepdog Society or the Kennel Club. Certainly, devoting a chapter to a breed which does not technically exist warrants some pretty convincing explanation.

Today a dog of similar appearance to a border collie, yet called a Welsh collie, is in fact frequently a border collie which happens to have been bred in Wales of Welsh parents. The border collie varies considerably in type from region to region and as a rule the Welsh strain is lighter in bone and smaller in build. The fact that Wales was the host country for the early sheepdog trials, a new country pursuit which was gaining great popularity in the latter part of the nineteenth century, may have accounted for why the general public connected the collie with Wales, even though many of the early winners were actually collies from Scotland. The Welsh have a great gift for discovering something good and laying claim to it – the corgi is another example of this.

As Harries McCulloch puts it in his book *Sheep Dogs and their Masters* (my edition is that of 1938):

> As mentioned previously, one might conclude from reading the history of Sheep-dog Trials, that clever dogs of the Border collie type had existed in Wales for centuries. That, however, was not the case. The first Collies were introduced into the Principality about 1830, and they came from Scotland. Prior to that the Welsh shepherds used dogs that were little better than curs.

He then goes on to tell of an interview he had with Mr Frank Thomas of Welfield, Builth, a Welshman who was considered an authority on shepherd dogs. He told him that a man named Lewis of Neuddn Rhayader was the first man in Wales to procure a collie from Scotland, and that was prior to 1828.

Recently, Mr Ruell of Builth Wells gave me some detailed information on the famous wild white bitch of Wales, said to be the first collie to come to the Principality. He writes:

> The 'white bitch' is supposed to have come to Wales when a gentleman from Scotland was competing in a large trial at Cardiff. His two dogs were travelling by train, and at the change of train at Builth Road station they both escaped. The one was recaptured but he failed to track down the white bitch.
>
> She was sighted by local people on the Doldowlodd, Llanafan and Cwmdaddhur hills and was eventually found in a rabbit earth on the Abergwepen range with a litter of puppies. The farmer took her home and nursed her back to health and managed to rear at least some of the litter. These puppies turned out very well and the white bitch went on to breed many more working dogs, but is believed to have never worked again herself.

> My personal knowledge of the breed is when a neighbour had one of her descendants which he had difficulty in handling owing to it being too hard. I had this dog off him and when trained, found it to be a very very good dog.
>
> One old dog, 'Mon' by name, belonging to Mr H. Jones, of Llanerchyrfe, a son of the old white bitch, in his day was considered the best dog for all-round work.

Mr Thomas told Herries McCulloch that he had introduced a good breed into the above district, which Mr Hope, of Abergwessin, has at the present moment. 'I took a good deal of trouble to get the breed in Scotland, and sent down to Wales a dog and a bitch; the dog last year took several prizes, beating all comers at Llanwrtyd.' Unfortunately he does not describe which breed he was referring to then, but one presumes it was a collie.

To give the impression that there were no truly Welsh sheepdogs would be wrong. Although most of the purely Welsh breeds are now extinct, this study would not be complete without some mention of their existence. In a few very isolated districts one comes into contact with some unusual types which the locals claim are the last of some ancient Welsh breed, and indeed there is no doubt that some very fine herding dogs of ancient lineage have existed in Wales. It is more likely that they were known as sheepdogs or hillmen, or by some other local name, not as collies. The Bydonic Celts of Wales were a different race of peoples from those in Ireland and spoke a Gaelic dialect which did not include the word collie.

The Welsh hillman

Today on remote farms in certain districts of Wales are to be found a number of good working dogs called by a variety of names. Among these are a few of the now almost extinct Welsh hillman type. He is a smooth-coated, usually brindle-coloured dog, high on the leg, and said to be extremely useful in the management of Welsh cattle.

One or two farmers have tried to revive the breed but the difficulty has been to find suitable breeding stock. A few people from outside the farming world who have owned bitches, declared by farmers to be the true hillman, not realizing they were such an old and rare breed, have had them spayed for convenience.

According to James Bourchier they were probably brought to Wales by the Phoenicians with the herds of goats from North Africa. A similar type is still used by tribesmen in the mountainous regions of that part of the world. The Romans were also thought to have brought a similar type from North Africa.

The old Welsh grey

He was a shaggy drover's dog, similar in type to those found all along the western side of Britain from Wales to Scotland, and certainly from the same ancestry. It is thought that these are now extinct or that they may have emerged as the beardie.

The Welsh blue grey

This is a purely local strain found on very few farms in Wales today. In appearance it resembles the modern border collie, but the coat can be best described as a beautiful slate-blue haze all over the body. They are regarded as exceptionally good workers, but it is doubtful if there is sufficient stock for them to be considered of importance as a separate strain.

The black and tan

According to Clifford Hubbard this breed, unfortunately now extinct, was probably one of the oldest in Wales, and my own researches have led me to believe that these may have been one branch of the ancestral line of the Lancashire heeler. Some even go so far as to say that he is one of the old ancestors of the Manchester terrier.

12

The Collie of Ireland

Until recent times cattle have been of more importance than sheep in the Irish livestock market, but the collie has always been a versatile farm dog. It is from the history of the Celts in Ireland that I have been able to trace what are possibly the most ancient herding dogs in the British Isles.

Three distinct Celtic groups occupied Ireland between the fifth and first centuries BC. The Cruthins arrived prior to 500 BC, followed by the Erainns and the Goidils. Each group lived in isolated communities but spoke a common Gaelic dialect, which was known as 'Q Celtic', from which the word collie, meaning 'useful', is derived.

The homes of these peoples were earthen structures, and agriculture and the raising of livestock were their main occupations; their herds and flocks were small, but it is known that specially trained dogs were kept to ward off attempts by wild animals to attack the lone herdsman and his stock while grazing, or the farmer tilling his land. These dogs were probably descended from those used by the Basque Celts, for they were of medium height with lithe, athletic bodies covered by a dense, harsh coat usually brindle in colour. The Irish zoologist W. L. C. Martin described them as follows: 'Ears, erect or nearly so; Nose, pointed; Hair, long and often woolly; Form, robust and muscular; Aspect, more or less wolfish.'

22 Gort and Rea, Irish collies owned by Mr Kevin
Shaughnessy. *Photo*: Sigma Visuals

These dogs' method of working was to circle the flocks and
herds to keep them together; if the enemy approached it would
be kept at bay by the hypnotic power of their eye. They were
not trained to kill or attack, as such an act would only scatter
and endanger the flocks or herds or even force them to turn on
the animals they were protecting. Hunting dogs like the Irish
wolfhound were kept for this purpose, and Irish greyhounds to
supply the larders. The last wolf seen in Ireland was supposed
to have been shot on Wolf-Hill near Belfast by Arthur Upton
of Aughnabreack, but no date of this is given. Another report
says one was killed near Glenarn, County Kerry in 1710.

When the Goidil Celts made their way over to the Western Isles of Scotland, history recalls the impact of this invasion on the local population but gives no information on the state of agriculture or livestock. Later, however, as Christianity spread, so too did the use of a trained dog to help with livestock farming.

When the monks from Ireland founded the monasteries on the outer islands of Scotland and ran farms to supply the daily necessities of life, they brought with them their own livestock and the labour to look after them. We learn a great deal about this from the travels of St Patrick, who was himself an agricultural worker in his youth. These monks fully appreciated the value of a well-trained dog for whatever purpose. So for the first time the true 'collie' arrived in Scotland from Ireland.

Viking influence was also a force to be reckoned with in Ireland as elsewhere, and in the provinces of Ulster, Munster and Connaught a type of pastoral dog has existed for centuries similar in size and build to those found in Scotland, thought by some to have been brought by the Vikings as guards for the herds and flocks. They were usually black and tan or sand-coloured with white or brindle markings, and rough- or smooth-coated. In character they were aloof and apprehensive, but loyal, trustworthy and intelligent.

In the province of Leinster, particularly in Co. Wicklow, is found a pure strain similar in appearance to a modern border collie, though slightly larger. Long ago they were born either with a natural bob or stumpy tail. Originally they were mainly red and white in colour or red merle, sometimes black and white, or an attractive sable or sandy colour with black points. They were strong but extremely tractable, and a very versatile stock dog. Much of their original appearance has been lost as a result of crossing with other breeds, the feature of the stumpy tail having practically disappeared, and the colour is now more frequently black and white. They are plain workers with not much 'eye' and inclined to be noisy, but they are powerful with large numbers of sheep, and very useful stock or yard dogs.

From customs records it appears that a few sheepdogs arrived in Ireland with the merino sheep from Spain and Portugal in the early part of the eighteenth century. The sheep from that area were being exported all over the world to effect improvement in local breeds. They were first brought to Wicklow to mix with the local cottagh breed, but the experiment was a failure as they disliked the wet and cold of the Wicklow hills. In this instance there is no mention of any 'foreign' dogs being brought over with them to usurp the supremacy of those famous Wicklow collies, which are also found in many other parts of Ireland and are a registered breed with the Irish Kennel Club.

Another type is the Iberian strain, as it was known, and which is thought by some to have been brought to the Irish monastery farms by monks returning from Spain and Portugal. This theory is disputed by others who say the dogs from that area were used only as guards of the flocks and trained to remain behind to guard stragglers as well. Whichever view is correct, we know that many found their way on to Irish soil in another way.

Smuggling was a way of life all along the west coast of Ireland as elsewhere along our coastline. Shipments of wool found their way to France and Belgium, and Spanish merino sheep, the breed that was fast becoming popular all over Europe, made illegal entry into Ireland together with a a few sheepdogs accustomed to working the herd. These were smuggled by the crews as tiny pups, along with lambs. During the voyage a relationship of trust built up between the dogs and the crew members, and many pups, together with small numbers of the imported lambs, adapted quickly when they arrived on remote Irish farms, and when trained made excellent stock dogs.

One interesting tale relating to a legal import of Spanish sheep into the province of Munster concerns Messrs Nolan of Kilkenny. It seems that by 1820 these gentlemen had imported upwards of 600 merinos from Spain together with a shepherd, who would not allow a dog on the farm. All his shepherding was conducted on horseback with the aid of a horn, and the leading sheep were trained to come to him by blasts on it in the same way that the shepherd whistles his dog today. These sheep were rewarded with a handful of salt (*The Farmer's Magazine*, 1820).

A number of Irish collies were taken to Australia, but it is not known from which strain, and little is known of their progress out there. Then we find an Iberian strain of pastoral dog turning up in America under the name of the Australian bob or shepherd. Such a breed has not been heard of in that part of the globe, but then this is an Irish tale!

Commercial or business acumen are not qualities for which the Irish are renowned but they know a good animal and its potential when they see one, and here were two, the sheep and the dog from which it was felt pure strains could result. Good cattle and horses raised on the wonderful pastures of Ireland have always been principal exports, while sheep and their by-products of wool and milk were raised mostly for home consumption.

The spinning and weaving of wool in Ireland had always been no more than a cottage industry supplying local needs, and the quality of the fleeces did not compare with those in England. In the sheep-rearing districts, particularly Galway and Roscommon, these new merinos and one or two breeds imported from England improved the quality of both fleece and flesh.

It would appear from early farming history that this improvement took place over a period of about 100 years, and during this time the imported dogs, by now called by the Gaelic name of collie, became a strain of useful farm dog and were being bred as carefully as the Irish greyhound or Connemara pony. Their fame had spread and it was not unusual for a shepherd from one of the big estates attending the fairs to persuade a farmer to sell him one of these collies for which a good price was paid. It is interesting that Ballinasloe fair, the biggest in the country and originally a wool sale, allowed no dogs in the vicinity.

When sheep or wool in England became scarce due to some local disaster or disease, and prices rose in consequence, then graziers and market dealers went to the fairs in Ireland where livestock was cheaper (see chapter 8 on Lancashire heelers) and all were impressed with the strength and beauty of the collies they saw both at the fairs and working in the fields.

By the beginning of the nineteenth century, the Iberian strain had been crossed with Scottish dogs and the results were seen working on almost every farm in Ireland and with all types of livestock. Many were brought over to work on big estates in England, particularly those where the owners had property in Ireland as well. Most of the collies on Irish farms today are of the border collie type, but on a few isolated farms in west Galway and Co. Clare one or two Irish collies can still be found.

A few dogs from a famous Irish strain bred for some time in Co. Monaghan, were brought over by a Mr Shirley to his English estate in Gloucestershire. When subsequently exhibited at English shows these dogs made a great impact for their beauty, and are the original ancestors of today's show collies. I am most grateful to Dr Jim Phillpotts, an Irishman who has had a lifetime's experience with these dogs, for reminding me of many of the aspects I have mentioned about them in this chapter. As I said at the beginning of the book I have searched for a new angle or a new light on all our herding breeds and more of this aspect is given in this particular case in the chapter on the rough-coated show collie.

Many years ago I crossed a rough-coated sable show champion with a black-and-white working border collie. In the resulting litter of five, all but one were black, white and tan and the other was sable and white. All went to farmers and proved excellent stock dogs and when mature could not have been distinguished from the Irish collies of the type illustrated here. There is a distinction in all collie varieties between a tricolour and a black, white and tan. The tricolours always have the tan spots above the eyebrows and the tan colouring is usually richer: most of the early collie types were black and tan only, but most of the Irish collies were sable or red and white, or brindle.

13

The Old English Sheepdog
or Bobtail

While I was collecting the material for the history of this remarkable breed, it occurred to me that a great deal of the information given in the first four chapters of this book also belongs here, for I am convinced that these dogs are descended from the ancient shepherds' mastiffs. Over the centuries, as a result of the differing requirements of the shepherds and the changing pattern of livestock farming, the role of this particular dog has altered, and when he was no longer needed by those shepherds of the higher order he became the useful aide of farmers, herdsmen and drovers.

Herding dogs of similar appearance were brought to southern England by farmers from the Continent as far back as 2500 BC, and types similar to the bobtail and the beardie are still found in areas both north and south of the Pyrenees. Dogs of this type became so much part of the lives of all ranks of the social order as guards, companions, hunters or herders that they became as commonplace as the horse and the ox. 'Familiarity breeds contempt', and sadly he was not held in high regard. Certainly, from the middle ages, the bobtail, whether French, Welsh or English, became a purpose-bred dog, particularly useful in areas where large flocks of sheep grazed on the meadows. Because of his build, his colouring which often blended with that of the flock, and his slow movement, he would be less likely to frighten the sheep, and as he was not too distinguishable from the flocks themselves, a thief or predator who happened too near could get a nasty shock when pounced upon by a vicious snarling 'sheep'. When sheep were later 'folded' (a fold or pen is a movable enclosure for holding sheep for a limited period) he was very useful, but it was as a yard dog or long-distance drover's dog that he was most widely used.

No doubt the laws of the forest and the tax from which the shepherd's dogs were exempt, helped to distinguish the bobtail from lesser curs and mongrels, and by the eleventh century a dog of similar description, either with or without a tail, was to be found on almost every farm in England. Lack of transport and a close-knit rural community stimulated the evolution of pure strains suited to the different districts.

Bobtails excelled as butchers' or drovers' dogs, and were trained for specific tasks on the drives, some to lead the flocks, some to drive from behind, while the others flanked the flocks or herds as challengers. They had no equal as guard dogs or yard dogs on the farms and in the stack yards, where any tres-passer, whether man or beast, was regarded as fair game for attack. I have been told this by several farmers whose fathers and grandfathers ran sheep on the Wiltshire Downs and Romney and Kent Marshes and used this type of dog to bring stock to the markets. Evidently they were also particularly useful at washing or shearing times, when a strong dog was needed. Before dipping became compulsory sheep were washed in the rivers, at certain appointed places, to improve the fleece before clipping.

The lighter types of sheepdog were not much used in southern England until about the end of the eighteenth century. In *The Dog* (1879) William Youatt quotes Richardson as declaring in 1850 that the shepherd's dog of England was the largest, the stronger and had much the appearance of a cross with a great rough water dog. It was coarser in the muzzle and coat and was destitute of tail. One cannot be sure though whether he was describing a gentleman shepherd's dog or a herdsman's dog! I can only presume that the Richardson referred to was John Richardson, the zoologist who made a study of the origins of many dogs of many countries.

The illustration of an 'English sheepdog' in the same book is the ugliest, meanest looking animal I have ever set eyes upon! It would be quite impossible to detect whether or not he has a tail and certainly he bears little resemblance to the shepherd's mastiff or drover's dog.

Many historians credit Gainsborough's painting of the Duke of Buccleuch with his dog of 1770, as being the earliest illustration of the breed, but my own findings do not tally with this assumption because I find the claim that the dog the Duke is embracing is a Dandie Dinmont more convincing. At that time this Scottish breed was in fashion, being equally acceptable as a companion dog in the castles of the lairds and as a sporting dog on the estates. It was for the portrait of the Duke and not of the dog that Gainsborough was being paid; even allowing for artist's licence, a smelly farm dog would hardly have fitted the image, but to exaggerate the proportions of the dog gave a more sportsmanlike composition, or possibly the Dandie was bigger in those days.

The Reinagle painting of the shepherd's dog of 1804 has also been claimed as an early illustration of the breed and indeed for several other herding dogs too, but it is clear from references in the *Sportsman's Cabinet* where the illustration appears, that he is the dog which fulfils the role of guard. The illustration and relevant information on shepherds' dogs appear in different parts of the book, which is confusing, but as much of it is really only wild speculation, I looked elsewhere for real information on this dog.

No significant progress appeared to be made in the breed for the next ten years, but during that time more country gentlemen were taking an interest in it, one such being Mr Richard Lloyd Price on whose estate in Bala in North Wales the first organized sheepdog trials were held. He was a well-known breeder of Old English sheepdogs, his grandfather having purchased the original stock from farms on the South Downs. In 1888 the first breed club was founded, but to whom or at what date we can attribute the development of local strains or types of these olde English dogges into a fixed breed remains a mystery. However, the fact remains that this humble herdsman's dog did eventually acquire a new status, and to add further to his new aristocratic image, the registered names given by the owners to males were prefixed by Sir and those to females by Lady or Dame, which was all most appropriate.

The breed first appeared on the show bench at Islington in 1865 in general sheepdog classes, but it was not until the Birmingham show in 1873 that separate classes for 'sheepdog, short-tailed English' were scheduled, with only three entries and no further details. From 1877 until 1890 the dogs registered with the Kennel Club under the title of Old English sheepdog were accepted as a true breed. Only two were entered in the first year: both were named Bob, pedigree unknown; one belonged to Mr Aggriss and the other to the Marquis of Blandford.

With increasing royal and public interest in our herding dogs as companions and show dogs, those who ran big kennels as a business saw a future in this breed. Their scouts could be found standing around the loading and unloading bays at country markets, prepared to offer a small but tempting price for a well-made dog of this type. When a likely purchase was spotted the scout could be seen gingerly running his hands along the back to the tail, to ascertain if it had a natural bob or a docked stump, as a few lines did produce the natural bob. If the latter was the case and his hand remained undamaged, for some of these dogs were very vicious and bad tempered, mainly as a result of ill-treatment and neglect, the scout would then offer some ridiculously low price, and much haggling followed, equal to that which regularly took place in the livestock pens.

It was not too difficult for an experienced breeder to detect if the tail stump was natural or docked. Docking of dogs was not carried out as skilfully as it is today, and the scars of such a mutilation could easily be felt. Spotting a well-made animal was not too difficult either, as most on view were either pups, not in full coat, or older dogs clipped out – quite a usual procedure both for a tidy appearance and on hygienic grounds. Neglected coats can become just as maggoty or pest-infected as a sheep's fleece.

Many of the early contributions on the breed, like those in the *Sportsman's Cabinet* and county journals of the early nineteenth century, were from the pens of self-opinionated, pompous gentlemen writing in scathing and condescending tones – a fashionable brand of journalism at the time, their way of concealing lack of practical knowledge of the subject.

Rawdon B. Lee was one such gentleman. Before he embarked upon writing books on dogs he was a journalist on the *Kendal Mercury* of which he was editor for a time. In 1830 he became the Kennel Editor of *The Field*, which gave him ample opportunity to meet kennel journalists from all over the world and to read their contributions, some of which were scathing in the extreme about our English bobtails, while others took a different attitude to this type of herder. All this publicity caught the imagination of American visitors who were anxious to see these 'creators of such derision', and were subsequently captivated by the 'rugged quaintness' of ye olde Englische sheepdog. The result was that from 1873, when the breed first appeared on the show bench, its success as a show and companion dog was assured on both sides of the Atlantic.

The popularity of the breed today is beyond question, but it is both interesting and amusing to read what Rawdon Lee wrote of it in *The Collie or Sheepdog, 1890*. Under bobtails he states:

There appears to be considerable difference of opinion as to the reputation that the old fashioned, bob-tail, rough coated, English sheep or drovers' dog ought to bear. His admirers praise his docility and intelligence and rave about the beauty of 'his bright blue eyes' and the rugged luxury of his heavy jacket. His detractors say he is a fraud and a deception, ugly to the mind educated to beauty, and by no means either as docile or intelligent as a guardian of the flocks and herds should be. As a fact the Collie Club refuses altogether to acknowledge him, so he is left to the tender mercies of a few enthusiastic admirers who formed a special club of their own to promote and foster their fancy, and it will be the fault of the public rather than of themselves if the BOBTAILED SHEEPDOG does not blossom into fashionable beauty.

Now we know that this is exactly what has happened, though some would say this cosmetic beauty treatment has now gone too far and his ruggedness is lost. 'Idestone', writing in a country journal, described the bobtail as follows: 'The English sheepdogs are slower and heavier than the Collie, blue-grizzled, rough-haired, large-limbed, surly, small-eared, leggy, bobtailed dogs, found chiefly in Oxfordshire, Wiltshire, Berkshire, Hants and Dorset.' He continues: 'They would obey no lighter instrument of punishment than the iron-shod crook, listen to no voice unless seasoned with a strong provincial twang, and coil himself up on none other than the inevitable drab blanket coat into whose sleeves no shepherd was ever known to put his arms.'

In his chapter on smooth sheepdogs James Watson (1906)

strays from his subject to give us the following information on the bobtail:

> We must, in order to disentangle the muddle into which the breeds have got, touch upon the writings of recent dog book editors in the chapters they have written upon the bobtailed dog. The mistake all have made is in taking it for granted that because some enthusiasts who formed a club in 1888 for the bobtailed dog gave it the name of Old English Sheepdog, that it was the original sheepdog, whereas it is a comparatively modern variety.

I am in no position to argue about his theory, but I do feel that it was only the new type emerging as an exhibition dog that could be called 'modern'. Interestingly, I have often found several references to smooth sheepdogs, along with those to the bobtail, in the same paragraph. I wonder if these references are to the dogs when they were clipped out, as most farm dogs were for reasons of hygiene, or to a smooth-coated variety, or to smooth-coated sheepdogs in general.

Further on in the chapter Watson states that 'most shepherds' dogs came under the name of Mastiff, and that the name is now accepted as nothing but an old English word for mongrel, and not in any way indicative of size, bulk or confined to the large dog we now call a Mastiff'. Part of his statement I would agree with, but according to my own researches it is somewhat contradictory, and my remarks in the chapter on forest dogs may shed some light here.

A full study of this theory, bearing in mind that the same role was played by his continental ancestors, presents a strong case for believing that the English sheepdog originated from these old sheep herdsmen's dogs, the name later becoming corrupted into shepherd's dog or sheepdog. Taking into account the language of the day it would not be difficult to see how later this became 'ye olde English sheepdog'.

23 Sir Cavendish, an original show type of Old English
sheepdog, drawing by Arthur Wardle.

Good early examples of the new fixed pure breed were bred
in Wales and Gloucestershire, but it was in the counties of
Norfolk and Suffolk that the first famous show champions
were bred (many having been created Baronets, Knights or
Dames by that time), and Dr Edwardes-Ker of Norwich was
responsible for breeding many early show winners.

The earliest names I can trace are Jockey, described as a
smooth dog, with a wonderfully thick, short, weatherproof
jacket, like long plush. He was a yellow sable, yet he produced
pigeon-blue stock. The other dog was Bob, belonging to Mr
Lloyd Price, who won second prize at the show in Birmingham, the first prize being withheld due to lack of quality.

143

Then there are the titled Sir Caradoc, Sir Guy, Dame Margery and Dame Ruth. Dame Margery came from a strain that continually produced three remarkable features. She was a beautiful blue colour and had a natural stump or bob and double dew claws on both hind legs, a feature frequently found in breeds from snow-covered or rocky regions. She was bought in Norwich market for half-a-crown and proved a profitable brood bitch. When mated to Jockey she produced two pups at fourteen years old, one being Sir Caradoc, the sire of the very famous Sir Cavendish, whose dam was Dame Ruth. Sir Guy was a half-brother to Jockey and when mated earlier to Dame Margery produced another Sir Guy with all the same qualities, but who was not so successful as a stud dog.

24   Brinkley Summertimes Blues, a modern Old English sheepdog owned by Mrs Tomes. *Photo*: Diane Pearce

Today most Old English sheepdogs are bred for exhibition or as companions, and only a very few are still used for work. Over the years the viciousness has been bred out of their character, the coat has become softer and more profuse, and the ambling gait so characteristic of this breed no longer seems to be an essential requirement. They need a lot of care and understanding but unfortunately can fall into the wrong hands, often as a direct result of commercial advertising.

14

The Shetland Sheepdog or Collie

The petite, pretty dog of today which most of us call the sheltie is the product of modern, very selective breeding, but the root stock of at least one ancestral line goes far back into history, as we saw in chapter 5. I have made an extensive study of the history, folklore and customs of the Shetland islands, and together with the help of my Scandinavian friends, this has enabled me to piece together some of the early history of these little dogs.

Until 1468 when the islands were handed over to Scotland, and indeed for some time afterwards, all trade and communication from the islands was with Scandinavia, not Scotland. The island economy relied mainly on sheep's wool, but also on fish, feathers and kelp, and the cottage industries created from these products.

There is no doubt that the specially bred and trained dogs originally brought to the islands for whatever purpose, were of the spitz or esquimaux type as they were more often called. All appeared to be well-balanced dogs with short legs, long bodies and square broad heads, strong jaws and good muzzles, although no doubt the shape of the feet and the length of the leg varied according to the nature of the work involved.

In his book *Ten Years in Sweden* (1865), Horace William Wheelwright describes the landscape, climate, domestic life, forests, mines, agriculture, field sports and fauna of Scandinavia, and gives the following information with regard to the native dogs:

> The only form of hound peculiar to the land which I know of are the Dahlbo-hound (now nearly extinct), a magnificent dog, rather like an English mastiff, of the size and colour of a wolf, which was formerly much used in the forests to watch the cattle when pasturing in the forests; the little bear hounds, not unlike the Esquimaux hounds, are peculiar to the north; and the Lap hounds, used for tending the reindeer on the fells, are mangy, ugly little curs, unlike any breed I have ever seen before.

The word hound or hund is the Continental term for any canine, and does not refer to a true hunting hound as we know it. Just as the collie was the useful versatile farm dog of Ireland and Scotland, so too was the vallhund of Sweden and the tun dogs of Norway. (Tun is pronounced 'toon', hence 'toonie dogs', a name given to them at one time.)

The dahlbo and the bear dogs probably worked as a team, as did the deerhounds and foresters' collies of Scotland, until the invention of the rifle made the role of the former and that of the dahlbohund redundant. Translations from the Scandinavian are sometimes a little difficult to follow, but it appears that until recently a few remaining dogs of these breeds were found in the districts of Dalsland and Västergotland and were only used very locally.

Photographs of the dahlbohunds show them to be large dogs something like a cross between a wolfhound and Bernese mountain dog, while the tun dogs appear to have a corgi-like appearance, though higher on the leg. Dahlbohunds are only of passing interest to us here, but the other half of the team continues to perform its useful noisy task of alerting both livestock and owners to any threat of danger. The instinct to guard and alert is still very strong in a modern sheltie.

People who have not visited the Scandinavian countries tend to think only of the fjords and inlets teeming with fish and wild birds, the pine forests full of reindeer, the snow-capped mountains and frozen lakes. But further to these breath-taking wonders, wherever there is any land suitable for farming, the systems of crop and animal husbandry are second to none, and all the natural resources are exploited to the full.

In Norway the livestock is housed during the long winter months in tuns or farmyards constructed in the form of a square, all the covered buildings facing an open yard, usually with a tree in the middle. During the summer months the stock is driven into the forests or to higher grazing in order to leave the lush lower slopes free for the cultivation of hay and other crops. The small, hardy, noisy tun or farm dogs were very useful for a variety of seasonal herding tasks around the tuns, but in the summer their main task was to keep the livestock on the higher grazing and give warning of any threat of danger.

The early Scandinavian families emigrating to the Zetland (Shetland) group of islands brought their own way of life, livestock and farming methods, but there the threat to their livestock was not from forest animals like bears or wolves, but from gulls, eagles and other birds of prey to which young lambs were especially vulnerable, there being very little natural shelter on the islands. With no fencing or natural barriers it was also essential to guard the cropfields and vegetable patches from human or animal trespass, so this was a part of the dogs' daily tasks, as well as assisting with the seasonal herding events.

There can be no doubt that herding dogs existed on the islands at least from the ninth century, probably very inbred or crossed with the local wildfowlers' dogs, but there is no recorded history to give any information on them. By the fifteenth century trade and communications between the islands and Scotland had expanded, and many crofters and their families had moved to the islands from the Scottish mainland, the Norse influence and way of life thus slowly becoming integrated with that of the crofters. No doubt in due course the collies they brought with them interbred with whatever local dogs were on the islands, and in time a local strain became established.

Between the fifteenth and nineteenth centuries there appears to be a lull or a gap in the historical development of the island dogs. Judging from the pictures of the island dogs, when we met up with them again at the beginning of this century it was obvious that the mainland working collie had a significant effect on changing the island types. The big change came when the blood of the 'improved' or show type pedigree collie was introduced.

Margaret Osborne, probably the best-informed authority on collie and sheltie lines and families, traces the roots of these island dogs from about this stage in her book *The Shetland Sheepdog*, first published as *The Popular Shetland Sheepdog* in 1959 and subsequently in seven editions. She tells us that at one time these dogs were known as the 'peerie' or fairy dog, and she feels the description of a sheltie as a fairy is most apt. I fully agree, but personally prefer her own delightful description of this modern breed as that of 'a collie viewed through the wrong end of a telescope'.

A remark by an elderly spectator at the International Sheepdog Trials at Lockerbie in Scotland in 1974, which I followed up, probably comes nearest to being an authentic record of how the modern sheltie evolved from the old island types. I have checked his story with letters and articles written in the country journals and canine magazines of the time, and have found no reason to doubt that it is true, in fact much of his information is borne out in the extracts at the end of this chapter.

Herding Dogs

Browsing through some doggie books on my stall at the trials was a lady with a charming little modern sheltie at her heels. We fell into conversation and presently I noted a real country character eyeing her little dog and listening intently to our chatter. She turned round to find him pointing his stick rather menacingly at the dog saying, 'I knew the old rogue what invented t'wee beastie.' (A wee beastie is in fact a term of endearment in Scotland.) The lady whispered to me, 'I think he's drunk,' and fled, rather to my relief.

The voice came from under a huge cap which sat on top of a small face like a shrivelled apple, studded with two bright blue twinkling eyes. The frame inside the Sunday best tweed suit looked as if it was constructed of wire mesh, and stood on a pair of well-polished boots, supported by a stout stick. Something suddenly clicked in my head, and I was anxious to get into conversation with this gentleman, drunk or not, for I felt that if he were genuine, he might be able to give me a clue to some of the mystery surrounding these dogs. Any information might be useful and I calculated that he was definitely not drunk and seemed willing to talk, but how should I make the opening gambit and what form should it take? One wrong move now and he might walk away.

Tom and I were combining work with a few days' holiday in our caravan on the trial grounds, so I suggested that he might like to join us for a cup of tea or a wee dram; this seemed an appropriate move for he accepted readily. Settling for a cup of tea, he seated himself awkwardly beside Tom on the edge of the caravan bunk, and pushed his cap to the back of his head, his body bent forward with hands still clasping the shepherd's stick which he had now placed between his legs. Meantime I busied myself at the stove, desperately searching for some remark to establish confidence and draw the old man out on the subject. I began, 'Do you come from the islands?' 'Ay' was the reply. 'Are you a competitor here?' I continued. 'Nay, just spectating,' was the answer. I sensed this line of approach was not going to get me very far.

Tom told him that he had visited the islands when he was on leave from France during the First World War, as his brother was serving in HMS *Warspite* at that time in Scapa Flow in the Orkneys and the War Office had given special permission for this sort of visit. Tom's reminiscences had a magical effect in stimulating an exchange between the two of them, but the problem now was how to steer the conversation back to the 'wee' dogs.

While our guest was sipping his tea I ventured, 'You were going to tell me more about the little dog you were looking at outside' – something told me not to give it a name. 'Oh aye, mind ye,' he drawled, ''twas a long teem ago.'

At a guess the man was over eighty years of age, so when he started talking about 'the old rogue' that he and his father used to visit when he was a lad, I gathered this must have been before the First World War. It seemed his father had a small croft on Shetland with a fair-sized dwelling house, and his mother took in summer guests. An old and most unscrupulous crofter-cum-drover/dealer lived on an adjoining croft which he farmed very unsuccessfully, but he made his living as a dealer and also as a casual farm hand and, as the old man put it, could turn 'muck into gold'. He also kept a few half-starved dogs which he always declared were the original island dogs, and his family were known to have kept that particular strain for generations. It seems the 'old rogue' took along his dogs whenever he obtained casual seasonal work on the farms, and they were very useful, but quite unlike any other dogs on the island.

Times were hard and puppies born on the farms or crofts were usually put down as soon as a litter was discovered, except occasionally if a pup was needed as a replacement, or they might be sold to holidaymakers. Our guest told me that one day 'some people, including a titled lady 'tis said' called at the farm and admired a litter of puppies, but remarked on the fact that they bore no resemblance to any breed she had seen before. The old dealer, never at a loss to turn any situation to his advantage, told the visitors that they were a rare, now almost extinct, native breed (which indeed most of the islanders believed to be true). That clinched it, the lady simply had to have one. My story-teller even recalled the purchase price.

He then told me that his father knew a commercial dog breeder of local fame in Lerwick by the name of Logie, who also ran an establishment for boarding the dogs of holiday-makers to the islands or from boats moored in the harbour. It seems the fame of the 'old rogue's' dogs both for their ancient lineage and their worth as workers could not be denied, so when Logie heard about the sale he contacted him, and after a lot of arguments, promises and hard bargaining, the two men finally came to an amicable and financial understanding about purchasing one or two of the remaining pups, which became known locally as 'Logie's toys'.

In those days pedigrees mattered very little and none were issued; parentage was always described as unknown. If any questions were asked the reply was always to the effect that crofters do not concern themselves with such things, all they care about is if the dog will do the job required, which apparently these dogs did. The old man gave me the impression that both James Logie and the 'old rogue' were genuine in their efforts to try to preserve these ancient island herding dogs, but where Logie went wrong was in giving them the title of the accepted Scottish term, collie. Even sheepdog, the title they were finally given, might have caused less controversy.

A few years later, in fact in 1908, Mr Logie, by then a well-known breeder of many breeds, including Logie Toys, suggested to a few enthusiastic folk that by forming a Shetland Collie Club they could share in his new-found gold mine, which they did. However, Logie then ran into trouble with various official bodies, so he packed his bags and emigrated to Australia, handing over all further interest to a Charlie Thompson from somewhere near Inverness in Scotland.

It was a great experience listening to this old man telling me all this, interspersed with local details, and I knew it had the unmistakable ring of truth. By the time Logie Toys, by now called Shetland collies, arrived on the show bench, the image of the rough-coated or 'improved' show collie was firmly implanted in the minds of both judges and exhibitors, so when presented with a miniature collie which looked nothing like a show bench collie of the day, they were at a loss to understand the 'wee beastie', and were scathing in their criticism of the exhibits.

Calling these dogs collies did indeed cause a lot of confusion. On one occasion two were registered by mistake at the Kennel Club as rough collies. Lerwick Floss was one – she gained a Second at Aberdeen Show in 1909 – the other was Lerwick Bess. Thomas Baker, a reporter for the magazine *Collie Folio*, gives the following report on her: '2nd prize Logie's Lerwick Floss (Fictor-Chloe), silky coat, ears carried like a spaniel, coat pale cream colour; of the Prince Charles type'. Many of the early winners on the show bench came from the Lerwick, Nesting and Inverness kennels.

The original genetic ingredients of this little 'shepherd's pie' will always remain a mystery, but we do know that among the ingredients for producing the final fixed breed were the genes of the 'improved' rough-coated show collie, and such breeding experiments are not without veterinary problems or loss of one quality to gain another. The limitation of size required by the present breed standard, plus the over-abundance of coat, would put the modern show sheltie at a disadvantage in carrying out most herding duties in the island terrain and climate, but given the opportunity, in the right hands and bred from the right lines – both points which must be stressed – some shelties are still capable of performing the tasks for which they were originally bred, and a few lines still do.

All praise to those early fanciers for continuing to strive for the recognition of the sheltie in the face of strong opposition, and in 1909 yet another club, the Shetland Collie Club of Scotland, with a Mr Forbes Grant as its President, was formed. It is not absolutely clear if James Logie's club was still in existence, but as can be noted in the extracts I give at the end of this chapter, the new club had very influential backing. In due course application for recognition was made to the Kennel Club in the name of both clubs: each submitted a form of breed standard, but both were refused.

Apart from cuttings in a scrap book, in my files are twenty-eight typed foolscap pages of letters and articles about the 'new' or 'old' breed from the Shetlands, which I have taken from magazines and journals from 1907 to 1913, many from the *Collie Folio*. Some of the outbursts in the articles, both for and against the introduction of the breed, are libellous in the extreme and obviously too lengthy to include here, but the few extracts which follow will give an idea of the fierce opposition to the word 'collie'. This was led by the editor of the *Collie Folio*, Mr W. E. Mason, who held the opinion that such a breed as a Shetland collie never existed, but by this time a strong body of influential opinion believed otherwise.

After long and heated arguments and some loss of friendship among the parties concerned, the Kennel Club eventually decided to grant the breed recognition under the title of Shetland sheepdog, but a great deal of opposition and controversy, even with regard to this recognition, still continued, and finally the whole case was referred to Theo Marples, editor of the canine weekly *Our Dogs*, for his independent advice. He felt the only safe course to take in order to avoid further antagonism all round was for the clubs to accept gracefully the recommended new Kennel Club title of Shetland sheepdog, which remains to this day.

An English Shetland Sheepdog Club was formed in 1919

25   Ch. Sharval Sandpiper, a Shetland sheepdog bred and
owned by Mr Albert Wright

putting forward yet another breed standard, but if the photographs are a true likeness, one could hardly apply any part of
today's standard to those early exhibits.

The dust of conflict has long since died down and from it has
emerged a really charming little dog, the delight of many
households and show benches, demonstrating that with care
and dedication and a measure of tolerance, breeders and exhibitors can make improvements on the original. The photograph
shown here to represent the modern show sheltie is of the dog
that set the final jewel in the sheltie crown when the Ch. Sandpiper of Sharval belonging to Mr Albert Wright became the first
ever Shetland sheepdog to win Best in Show at a Championship
Show, which he did at Belfast in September 1978, from an entry of
several thousand dogs of all breeds and varieties. To make the
win doubly sweet, both dog and owner hailed from Scotland.

When I first started on my scrapbook I had no idea that the newspaper cuttings and scraps of information which I had collected over the years would be of any historical value, so unfortunately I did not always record exactly in which paper or magazine they had been found, nor do I have a full collection of *Collie Folio*, but I have given such details as are known in the following extracts:

A press cutting from *Field and Fancy* (no date recorded):

The Shetland Sheepdog is gaining in strength in England, and this country may look for a few representatives before long. Reports from England say that they are in much greater demand than a year ago, and that prices are at least 50 per cent greater than was the case six months ago. In fact, many of the Collie fanciers on the other side are beginning to become alarmed at the reception being tendered this new breed. It is doubtful, however, if competition will become keen enough to warrant any great intrusion in the ranks of the Collie for sometime to come, and if there is any apprehension as to this it should be set aside, as it will be some time before the Shetlands will become established

From a press cutting in *Field and Fancy* (no date or author recorded):

I hear that the breeders on the island have a big demand for them, presumably to cross with small typical Collies. The result will be (and I shall, for one, welcome them) a miniature or toy Collie, and I will ask the Collie men, and especially those who are so bitterly crying it down, what could be more beautiful and delightful than a 'toy' Ch. Quality of Dunkirk or a champion Rough Collie in the miniature? If once they are produced small enough and

typical enough, and it should be a matter of only a few
generations, I am confident they will be most popular, and
when there is money in them their enemies of today will be
their friends of tomorrow, and those who start to make the
Shetland Collie what its name implies, a perfect miniature
of the species . . .

A newspaper cutting gives the following (signed Mr
William Thane of Kirkcaldy, N.B. 1908):

I should say, without hesitation, it is a cross between a
Pomeranian and a Toy Spaniel. I knew a man, employed
by a relation of mine, who bred those little Toys, and Lady
Marjorie Sinclair (who owns a kennel of them) often used
to try and buy puppies from him, and the sire of the
puppies was always a pure-bred Pom. The dam was
exactly like the Toy Collies that are now being exhibited –
Spaniel eyes, Pom's tail, bow-legged, curly-coat – and
every Toy fancier that saw this dog said it was a most
typical Shetland Collie.

Report from *Collie Folio*, July 1908, p. 206:

A pleasant show in a pleasant town on the banks of 'Father
Thames'. Collies were poor in numbers, and Bobtails were
cancelled. The most noticeable feature was the benching of
a pair of Shetland Toys, incorrectly labelled as 'miniature
collies'. These are the first we have seen exhibited in
England, and it is satisfactory to know they were entered
merely in the variety classes. More pronounced mongrels
we have never seen, and certainly they possess not a single
feature akin to the Collie. Owned by no less a personage
than The Lady Sybil Grant (daughter of the Earl of
Rosebery), who appears to have been informed that they
are a pure and distinct breed, though almost extinct. We

were told they represent what Collies were 50 years ago, and are very, very rare. Thank goodness they are, as they possess not a single attractive feature. Spaniel strain is evidenced in both, with, maybe, a Scottish Terrier an adjacent branch of their interesting genealogical tree.

Bandy-legged, goggle-eyed, flop-eared, apple-headed weeds, weighing from 8 to 12 lbs., with soft, silky coats best described these nondescripts, if the Irishism may be permitted. Neither breeder's name nor parents are known, yet we believe some person sold these animals at very high prices as good specimens of a rare breed. On the face of it, those responsible for the perpetration of such a fiasco ought to be asked to prove the statements used to effect the sale.

Collie Folio, January 1909, p. 15:

At a meeting held in the County Hall, Lerwick, recently, a club for the Shetland Collie was formed, and its list of patrons is a formidable one. Provost Porteous presided over the meeting and Lady Marjorie Sinclair, Mr Cathcart Wason, MP, Sir Arthur Nicolson, Mrs Moffat, and Mr Bruce were appointed patrons. Provost Porteous was made President, and the Rev. A. J. Campbell Vice President, while Baillie Laing is Chairman of Committee. Mr J. A. Logie is Treasurer and Secretary. Lady Marjorie Sinclair is, as everyone knows, a daughter of the Countess of Aberdeen, and has been a doggy enthusiast since her childhood. Mr Wason, who represents Shetland in Parliament, has taken a keen and personal interest in the Shetland Collie controversy, and is no mere figurehead. There is something peculiarly appropriate that the Shetland Collie Club should be formed in Lerwick, and, despite the weight of the opposition to the Shetlander as a show dog, there are surely few breeds that have got such an auspicious send-off in the matter of their specialist Club. Sassenachs beware!

The photograph of the 'Supposed' High Class Shetland Toy which appears elsewhere in this chapter was submitted by Thomas Baker.

Collie Folio, February 1909, p. 63:

That there are dogs containing Collie strain in Shetland, but not miniatures, may be the fact. Our informant learns from a regular visitor to the Shetlands that the dealers in dogs there obtain cast-off Pomeranians from Aberdeen to sell as Shetland Collies, which in all probability will be used to breed from and perpetuate this absurdity.

We give a few criticisms, furnished by our correspondent, of the dogs exhibited at Aberdeen Show . . .

The correspondent was Mr Thos. Baker

Fanciers' Gazette, 1909:

'The Shelty'

As one of the first Collie men in the West of Scotland, who was unfortunate enough to be called upon to adjudicate upon this nondescript, I should like to express my views. At the last City of Glasgow Kennel Club Show, where the entry numbered seven, but only five put in an appearance, in the two classes which were guaranteed, I made the awards. Of the five dogs shown there were four different types of cross-bred Toy dogs, but not one of – if such a thing exists – a Toy Collie. I have read a lot of piffle that has been written about the Shetland Collie, but, knowing the source from which it came, took no notice of it. And looked upon its author as merely writing for notoriety and the usual penny a line.

Collie Folio, February 1909, p. 69:

So far so good, and for the achievement of these mercies the entire fancy ought to be specially grateful to Mr W. Stephens, the Collie enthusiast and member of the Committee of the Kennel Club, Mr W. T. Horry, and Mr J. H. Jacques. We propose to purchase each a halo to be worn on state occasions.

The Kennel Club have further enacted that owners of these Toys who have erroneously registered them as Collies can re-register them under this new 'Any other variety class' free of charge. Scribes who have taken the view opposite to our own may now prepare a suitable memorial service in commemoration of their dear little idols, and no doubt we shall be treated to some clever wriggling. For the present, therefore, we leave the subject, but can promise a return to it if at any future time efforts are made to resuscitate the agitation which had for its objective such unworthy ideals.

15

The Bearded Collie or Beard

Part of the early history of this useful type of herdsman's dog before it became a pedigree fixed breed, is also to be found in the history of the drovers' and Smithfield dogs. Research into its origins, however, has presented more difficult problems. The variety of titles given to this type of dog ranges from Scotch, Highland or mountain collie to hairy mou-ed or shepherd's cur, depending upon the area in which one met him. Each title warranted separate research to try to establish his ancestry, and it has been both a fascinating and a frustrating exercise. Fascinating because it led me to discover so many facets of rural life one does not normally encounter, and frustrating because I could find no authenticated written reference of its real origin, just a few far-fetched speculations.

The writings of my great-uncle James Bourchier, who made an extensive study of European and North African herding dogs, gave me one possible clue to their ancestry. He believed that the shaggy types of the British Isles evolved from dogs brought over from North Africa by the Romans, like the Egyptian sheepdog, sometimes called armant, which comes from a district of that name in upper Egypt. When brought to England just after the First World War by the Egyptian Ambassador, one of these dogs created great interest, and according to an account in *The Field* those who saw him said he could not be distinguished from our own beardie types found near the English/Scottish border counties at that time.

It is interesting that the armant and a Pyrenean breed, the labrit, are very similar in appearance to our old beards, and both are found working on opposite shores of the Mediterranean. Few people have the opportunity to see the smaller Basque or Pyrenean breeds at work, but they do appear in the French show rings, and when groomed and trimmed, they look exactly like a smaller version of a beardie.

The beardie is also likened to the *berger de Brie* or *briard*, but in fact he is far more like the *berger de Pyrénées*, a real shepherd's working dog of which the labrit is one variety. These dogs must not be confused with the large white mountain dogs of the region, which were used only for guarding, not herding. There is also a Hungarian cattle dog called a pumi, very similar in appearance to a beardie, and he in turn must not be confused either with the Hungarian puli, a dog of totally different appearance. There are also shaggy types of herding dogs in Poland and other countries bordering the Baltic around the Gulf of Riga.

Other historians believe that he is descended from a shaggy type of herding dog brought to Britain by the Anglo-Saxon farming communities, and that possibly both the bobtail and the beardie share this same ancestry. I have mainly confined my study of his history and evolution to his role as drover's dog, in which capacity I dispute the assumption that he is related to the bobtail, for reasons I have given in chapter 4. Unfortunately, when the bearded type was being transformed into a fixed recognized breed, some bobtails were used. It is also claimed that this variety of collie is of ancient Scottish origin, but I do not accept this.

A few years ago the secretary of a sheepdog trial near Otterburn introduced me to a Northumberland farmer who was competing with his 'beard', as the locals called him; he gave me food for thought about origins. He had asked to meet me because of our mutual interest in old shepherding books. Regrettably, like so many with great stores of knowledge on these matters, he has since passed on, and his sons have forsaken farming. His family had bred and worked this variety on the local sheep runs together with a few terriers (for different purpose) for several generations.

During our conversation that bleak autumn afternoon he emphatically pointed out to me that there was no intercourse between England and Scotland until 1603 when James VI of Scotland became James I of England, and then it was not until almost a century later that trade in agriculture and livestock began to flourish between the two countries. Important historic events are never forgotten in the Border counties. This farmer said they may have been an ancient pastoral breed, but not of Scottish origin, for it was only since the early part of the nineteenth century that a pure strain of this type of herding dog became established over the Border, being descended from a strain of droving dog brought into Scotland from Wales and west of the Pennines about a century earlier. I later discovered he was referring to what were called the Galloway types.

It was obvious from our conversation that he had carefully studied his excellent collection of dog books, and also those on local farming history. He was most amusing – and often a little uncomplimentary – about those who concerned themselves with writing on pastoral dogs or other farming matters, and as we looked through some of his books we discussed the value of the information given about this type of dog. In particular, the references to Scotch or Highland collies in Edward Jesse's *Anecdotes of Dogs* (1846), as the title implies, must be treated with some scepticism. Reading through its pages one is aware that it is intended as a witty or fun book, written with tongue in

163

cheek, and that the information is at best misleading. In the *Sportsman's Cabinet*, vols. 1 and 2 (1803 and 1804), neither of which he had read he told me, the chapters or brief references to Scotch collies were written by sportsmen not involved in the shepherding scene and also make curious reading in places. As we have already seen, the Reinagle illustration often claimed for this breed has been claimed for several other breeds as well.

James Dalgliesh in his chapter on collies in Leighton's *The New Book of the Dog* (1907) refers to Scottish or Highland collies, but gives no history of the breed. He states that Peeble-shire was the true home of the beardie and that he had judged them at several pastoral shows in the area, adding that Sir Walter Thorburn, a patron of the breed, contributed prizes annually at three shows for the best bearded dogs owned by a shepherd. In fairness to this gentleman it should be pointed out that the editor Robert Leighton states in his Preface that he has 'altered, excised or amplified some of the chapters to bring them into literary harmony'; perhaps this was also the case here as he includes rough and smooth show collies under the same heading.

The Bearded Collie, a Foyles' handbook published in 1971 and written by the late Mrs Willison, was the first book about the breed. In it she made no extravagant claims about its early history, simply repeated the opinions of others while giving an account of the part her own dogs played in the breed's revival.

Personally, I have only come upon one or two beardie types in Peebleshire, and it is curious that I did not encounter any in the Highland regions of the north, although that is not to say there were none there. However, it gives some hint that the original title 'Highland' may in fact have referred to the Gallo-way Highlands, as I found more evidence of the breed on the west coast, and of course in the north-west of England, than elsewhere.

When researching in the Border counties of England, I frequently met shepherds working with a beardie type, some with stumpy- or bob-tails. They told me that this was the old-type drover's dog used for collecting livestock across the Border in either direction. I was also informed that he was a useful, strong market or butcher's dog. Before rail transport, graziers from the north of England made frequent trips to the Highlands with flocks of young sheep as replacements or for cross-breeding, returning with cattle and ponies and accompanied by – possibly local – dogs. Cattle, horses and ponies brought down by Yorkshire drovers are mentioned in many records, yet there is no description of the dogs, and without them, the journey could not have been accomplished. It is quite conceivable that the dogs taken on the outward journey were their own local dogs, familiar with the flocks, and local dogs familiar with the ways of wild cattle and ponies may have been used on the return journey. In the past dogs were bred and broken for this type of work and owed no allegiance to their masters, their essential qualities being a strong constitution and the ability to survive.

The rearing of Galloway horses and cattle in that region of Scotland had always been a specialized business, and horse breeding was an essential part of the economy of most farms. The ancestors of some lines of our Dale and Fell ponies can be traced back to the hardy ponies of Scotland, Galloway stallions being especially useful for crossing with local mares. Galloway cattle were regularly sent down to the lush pastures of Norfolk and Suffolk to be fattened, before being sent on to Smithfield market. It is known that the dogs that accompanied these droves were all of the droving beardie type; strong, determined dogs which later became known as Smithfield collies, they were bigger and longer on the leg than the beardie we see today.

Information of this nature gives great credibility to the theory that there were two strains, the Border, and the Highland or Galloway. A farmer in the mountain regions around

26   A group of beardie and border collies belonging to a
shepherd in Crammie, Glen Cora, Scotland

Craven, in the Eastern Dales of North Yorkshire, known
locally as the Craven Highlands, told me that the dogs used on
the local farms were described as 'Highlanders', and that those
used as shepherds' dogs were somewhat smaller than the
droving strains. The beardie and border types were frequently
cross-bred and the different working instincts of each type
seemed to complement each other in the offspring.

    In their delightful book, *Life and Traditions in the Yorkshire
Dales*, Marie Hartley and Joan Ingilby give us this amusing
little snippet.

    A Yorkshire grazier by the name of Birtwhistle, from 1795

onwards regularly brought cattle and ponies from
Scotland, and at times as many as 20,000 head of Scotch
cattle could be counted on his grazings near Malham in
Yorkshire. When crossing the border into England, he
employed a piper who headed the entourage all the way on
to their new grazing.

They also tell us that

The Pratts families in Upper Wensleydale regularly visited
Oban, Lanark, Sterling and the Islands in the first half of
the nineteenth century. A descendant, James Pratts (1852–
1927) of Burtersett, stayed at the Caledonian Hotel,
Lanark, for sixty consecutive years, visiting auction marts
and farms to buy Scotch cattle, shorthorns and sheep.
Until 1965 Mr E. Pratts continued to bring down cattle by
train from Scotland each spring and autumn.

We read elsewhere of lots of 40 to 100 cattle and any number
of up to 600 sheep being brought down together in September
along the old drove roads, walking 15 to 20 miles a day depending on the weather. Local drovers brought them as far as the
Border, resting at night in inns, farm buildings or caves, well
wrapped up in their plaids, and then others took over. For
those who hold strong beliefs that this is purely a Scottish
breed, then there is no doubt that the deerhound figures in the
family tree of the types found north of the Border. I feel the old
Welsh grey figures in the family tree of those from south of the
Border, but it was the beardie/border crossed types which were
the most useful, and they are still used on farms today.

In *The Deerhound* George Cupples mentions in several
places the usefulness of the deerhound/collie cross, but we are
left to guess which type of collie is meant. According to the hill
shepherds I have spoken to, both in Wales and Scotland, the
old-type beardie or shaggy dog was an excellent cattle dog, but

when an all-purpose dog was required they were crossed with the border collie types found in the Lowlands of Scotland and the Border counties of England. The temperament and qualities produced by these crosses seemed to complement each other so well that the resultant offspring were bred together for a further generation or two and then the process started again with fresh blood.

The crosses mentioned above produced two types of strains of beardie, one being black and white and referred to as the Border strain and the other being fawn, grey or brindle and referred to as the Highland strain. The former were very popular at early sheepdog trials. The Highland strain may be descended from the forest dogs or he may be the deerhound/ collie cross or indeed come from the strain found in the Galloway Highlands which were regarded as excellent hill dogs, possibly from an infusion of blood of each type.

Many early illustrations, entitled either the English bobtail, the Scotch bobtail or Scotch collie, all appeared very similar. It would be unlikely that an artist should see a working dog in natural full coat; when the sheep were clipped out or shorn, dipped or salved, so too were the sheepdogs, thus much would depend on the stage to which the coat had grown when the artist saw the dog.

Before chemical washes and insecticides came on to the market, sheep suffered one further indignity at the hands of man, that of being 'salved' in the early autumn. This involved rubbing the sheep over with a foul-smelling mixture of oils, tar and fats. The treatment acted as a pesticide and also as a valuable protective coating in bad winters or snowy conditions by holding the fleeces together, and the dogs also underwent the same treatment.

On some farms this practice was carried out until 1905 when the compulsory dipping order came into force. If a sheep has a long and heavy coat it parts with the weight of the snow, allowing the damp to penetrate into the underfur and often causing pneumonia. This can also happen to a heavy-coated dog, if not clipped or treated in some way. The dogs had a second application to the legs and belly at the onslaught of winter to prevent snow balling, a very necessary precaution when dogs are working in deep snowdrifts. A recipe given in one book for this mixture was one gallon of tar to 17 lb of butter – it is no wonder that farm dogs were not welcome in the house! The beardies seen in the ring today, with carefully groomed, long, textured coats, often parting down the centre back, due to excessive length, could never survive in the snows or heavy mists, but fortunately they no longer have to.

By the 1800s a definite fixed type had emerged in Scotland which was similar in appearance to the Welsh types, but said to be a selected strain from deerhound/collie crossing. This new Scottish beardie was more of a sheepdog than drover's dog. Beardies are not silent workers, nor do they work in the same manner as the border collie: they hunt and give tongue when approaching their quarry, which has the effect of causing sheep to herd together, and ewes and lambs to 'mother-up'. When the flock has gathered, then another dog, often a silent worker like the border collie, is sent up to bring the flock down from the hills.

To locate stray sheep away up on crags or mountainsides is very different from herding sheep on marsh or lowland grazing. Weather conditions in Scotland often make it impossible for a shepherd to see his flocks, but a team like this can gather and drive by sound and scent in almost all weather conditions. It can be appreciated that as hill dogs beardies were most useful, and as drovers' dog they were invaluable. When working as a team with border collies they were capable of gathering any livestock from remote areas and then holding the flocks or herds together day and night for the duration of the drive.

27   A Perthshire shepherd with two beardie/border crosses.
Photo: Bertram Unne

At the turn of the century, with the exception of a few registered with the International Sheepdog Society as working
sheepdogs, the beardie was threatened with extinction; its place
was being taken by the more fashionable border collie which
was gaining popularity in the trial field. The farmers, particularly in Scotland, who bred and used the beardie type, did not
trouble about pedigrees or breed points until the formation of
the International Sheepdog Society, and even then only a few
dogs were registered here as sheepdogs under rough, smooth
or beard-coat types. Shepherding was more to the liking of
beardie owners than competing at trials, which was both costly
and time-consuming.

Dr Russell Greig, a well-known Scottish veterinary

surgeon, had a great interest in Scottish working dogs. He felt the breed should not face extinction, so he set about founding the first bearded collie club in 1912 in Edinburgh, and a brief breed standard was drawn up. Unfortunately the club only survived for a few years and folded up after the outbreak of the First World War. No further attempts were made until 1930 when that great doggie personality Jimmy Garrow, together with Mrs Cameron Miller, tried once again to revive interest, but this project also faded out. It is not clear if the breed was recognized by the Kennel Club or indeed if application had been made at that time, but twenty-five years later the beard seemed to have slipped in quietly through the back door and became a pedigree-fixed breed with full Kennel Club recognition and has become very popular in the show and obedience ring. For this all praise must go to the late Mrs Willison who did so much in re-establishing the breed, partly through a chance meeting with Mrs Cruft, the wife of the man who gave his name to the most famous dog show in the world. Mrs Willison's original beardie bitch was bred in Scotland by a Mr McKie of Killiecrankie, and Mrs Cruft helped to locate a mate for her in Devon, so north and south met up to produce a litter that was to start the revival of this attractive herding dog, albeit in a new role.

Mrs Willison told me that in the early days of breeding beardies it was quite usual to find one or more pups in a litter which resembled border collies, no doubt a throw-back to the crosses I mentioned earlier. Since the beardie collie has become an exhibition dog, a study of his physical points has claimed the attention of breeders above all else, and he has become what is termed the 'improved' type. Working tests have been drawn up for owners who wish to participate, but these are more in the form of temperament and obedience tests and not a test of their ability to control any form of stock.

Here once again we have a case where, if a breed had not been

28 Gillaber Glendronach, a bearded collie owned by Mrs
Gill and Mrs Cook. *Photo*: Diane Pearce

taken up by the show fraternity, it could well have faded out. It
has inevitably altered, but so long as these dogs continue to give
people pleasure and companionship this is sufficient reward in
itself.

The Bearded Collie Club was founded by Mrs Willison in
1955, yet the inadequate breed standard drawn up in 1912 by
the defunct club in Scotland appears to have been the one in
force when bearded collies were granted championship status
by the Kennel Club in 1959. A Kennel Club breed standard was
issued in 1964 and altered in 1978, but it was not until 1972 that
the breed club held its first championship.

When the breed was first recognized, only a few exhibits
appeared at championship or open shows, but separate classes
for beardies were scheduled at other collie shows. The first

champion of the breed was Ch. Beauty Queen of Bothkennar, suitably named, bred and owned by Mrs Willison.

I remember judging the classes for the breed at a London Collie Club show in 1964. There were twelve entries in two separate classes, and all except one were sired by Bothkennar dogs. The Best of Breed on that occasion went to Miss M. A. Taffe's Heathermead Magic Moments.

At present there are two breed clubs with branches in various parts of the UK which give valuable information and help to owners, and there are also one or two good books catering for the modern history of the breed, exhibiting and general care (see Bibliography).

16

The Rough-coated Show Collie

The long-headed, profusely coated modern collies seen in the show ring today are not herding dogs in the true sense, in fact they have not been bred for that task for over 100 years, but their ancestry brings them into the herding or pastoral group. The breed is often incorrectly referred to as the Lassie collie, due to the popularity of the dog of that name in American story books and films.

When put to the test, any latent instincts to work livestock which may be visible in some of today's lines are due mainly to the ability or domestic circumstances of the owners. The rough-coated show collie first appeared as a separate breed on the Kennel Club register in 1895. Up to this time they were still regarded simply as farm colleys or sheepdogs of either coat, and their early history or family tree is the same as that of many of the herdsmen's dogs found all over the British Isles.

As I mentioned in a previous chapter there is no doubt that Mr Shirley and the strain of collies he bred at Lough Fea in Ireland, had a most important influence on the new line or breed of pedigree collie, but the appearance of collies in the show ring began in the early Victorian era, and in the chapter on Scotch collies I have given brief details of this early period of their show history. Hounds and sporting dogs have always been kept at royal kennels, but when Queen Victoria came to the throne in 1837 the intake of pastoral dogs and other breeds at the kennels at Windsor and Balmoral increased. The Queen loved all dogs, especially the smooth-coated collie, and many were presented to her. As the royal children grew up, they too inherited the love of the collie, particularly white collies. It was, however, Queen Alexandra, when she was still Princess of Wales, who popularized and made the new 'improved' rough collie fashionable. Is it any wonder that these dogs are called the aristocrats of collies?

A great deal of the information given in this brief history was supplied to me many years ago by Mr Southwell of Norfolk who served as a kennelman at Sandringham House, helping to

29   J. Emms, *Bobs*, a rough-coated show collie (1901), owned by Lady Sassoon

look after the various breeds of dog owned by Queen Alexandra and her family. As a boy he served under Mr Brunson,
the head kennelman seen in the background of the famous
painting of Queen Alexandra and her dogs by Morgan and
Binks, hanging in Sandringham House. He told me that several
of the royal dogs, including the collies the Queen exhibited
herself, had won various awards, and in fact these were listed in
the Kennel Club Stud Book, as are those of Queen Victoria and
the Prince of Wales. Mr Southwell told me that although
unplanned matings frequently occurred at the royal kennels,
very selective breeding also took place. It seems that the cross
between the collies and borzois produced beautiful puppies,
many of which were given away as pets and some exhibited.

The Czars and members of the Russian aristocracy brought
this type of dog as gifts when visiting our royal family, and it
was Mr Southwell's special job to look after them. He told me
that in an attempt to improve the stamina of the real hunting
borzois of Russia it was decided that as the crossing of collies
with gundogs had proved so successful an experiment it might
have the same effect on borzois which had become too inbred
in Russia. However, he pointed out that the collies selected
were from ordinary working stock, some on the Balmoral
estates. Unfortunately world events prevented us from following the progress of any offsprings taken back to Russia. Of
those remaining in this country the offspring produced a new
and more glamorous type of collie which Mr Southwell said
became known as the borzoi type.

It is claimed by many that this 'new improved' type of collie,
or the modern show collie – and I stress this qualification – is of
Scottish origin, but as pedigrees prove, this is not the case. One
wonders if it was modesty on the part of Mr Shirley or a case for
diplomacy on the part of the Kennel Club, that 'the improved'
collie was registered as the rough and smooth collie and not the
Irish collie. Indeed the first collie of note to win in the show

ring for which a pedigree was given was Shamrock belonging to Mr Shirley and of pure Irish ancestry, and it is this type which has made the most impact on the modern show collie.

Early historians of the breeds have chosen to ignore, or perhaps were not aware, that 'the Gaelic' is also the language of Ireland, and collie means the same there as it does in Scotland, 'useful farm dog'. These dogs, albeit a more thick-set type and smaller, with slightly leaner heads than the Scottish ones, have worked on the farms and hills of the Emerald Isle for centuries. It is thought that like some of the good wool-bearing breeds of sheep, they originated in the Iberian Peninsula. There is a lot of Spanish influence down the west coast of Ireland and also a good strain of herding dog, call them what you will. More information on the breed is given in chapter 12.

When Mr Shirley and his shepherd Mr Smith helped to organize the first sheepdog trials in 1873, which I cover in a previous chapter, reports and illustrations of the event in old copies of journals of the day gave me the first clue to search in pastures new for the history of the modern show collie.

As members of the International Sheep Dog Society, my husband and I attended the Centenary Trials at Bala in 1973, and sitting next to us in the stand was an old gentleman who told us that his father, who knew Mr Shirley, had attended the first trial held there in 1873. While Tom and the old gentleman were reminiscing, for this is one of the pleasures of these occasions, he told us that the collie in the foreground of an illustration of the Trial which appeared in the *London Graphic*, was in fact Bess, the dam of the famous Trefoil. She was bred by a Mr Glasby but owned by Mr Shirley's shepherd, Mr Smith.

He thought the dog in the foreground of another illustration in *The Field* was Twig, the sire of Trefoil, but I am of the opinion that it may have been the grandsire Shamrock and not Twig. It is known that Shamrock was being campaigned at English shows in 1873, as it is recorded that he won at Crystal

30 Trefoil, ancestor of all the modern show collies, owned by Mr Shirley, bred by his shepherds at Lough Fea, Ireland

Palace, Glasgow and Fakenham shows that year. If the sketches of the two dogs at the sheepdog trials are a true likeness, then I feel the sketch of Trefoil shows him to be altogether too big and cumbersome for this type of collie, but we must remember it is by a different artist and the only one so far known of the dog. Shamrock appears as No. 2897 in the Kennel Club Stud Book, owned by Mr Shirley, but bred in 1870 by a neighbour, Mr Glasby of Carrickmacross, and he was black, tan and white, by Mr McCall's Shep out of Mr Glasby's Bess. Mr Smith owned the grandsire of this bitch and when later mated to Twig she produced the famous Trefoil No. 4523 in the Stud Book. Neither Twig nor Bess appears in the Stud Book, so one presumes they were never shown, but it is interesting that her grand-dam was owned by Mr Johnstone, the steward at Longfield, Carrickmacross, and the great-grandparents were owned by Sir G. Foster of Stonehouse, Co. Louth, not far from Lough Fea, and therefore all Irish-bred.

The family tree of our modern show collies can be found in most of the collie books, so here I will mention only a few of special interest. Records show Cockie born in 1868 to be the first show collie of note. Followed two years after by Mec, both later being known as Old Cockie and Old Mec. In farming circles the prefix 'Old' is given to an animal when it has mature offspring, or as a term of endearment.

I found the following advertisement for Cockie in the *Fancier's Gazette* of 16 May 1874, but I am at a loss to understand some of the glory claimed for this dog. If the title of Champion could not be officially claimed until after 1880, I am not surprised that the gentleman writing in *The Field* questioned the exaggerated claims for this dog.

THE CHAMPION SCOTCH COLLEY

'COCKIE' AT STUD – This celebrated dog is winner of upwards of thirty prizes taken at the principal shows in the North and South of England. A few of his chief performances are prizes at Birmingham four years in succession, including the Cups in 1872 and 1873: first prize Maidstone and the Mayor's cup: first prize Border Counties Show 1870: and the Open Champion Colley Cup, beating seventy-four dogs (vide Mr Hetherington's letter in *The Field*, 14 March 1874), also first prize and cup for the best rough-coated Colley at Nottingham 1873. Cockie is a grand, well-proportioned dog, with a magnificent flag, well carried muscular loins, and the true type of head, ears, colour and coat. Photos 1s: large size, mounted 6s each – For further particulars, stud fee, &c

apply to owner, W. H. Johnson, High Bank House,
Eccles, Manchester.

Historians of the breed differ about the influence these dogs
have had on it. Some say 'Old Cockie' had a great influence,
others say that his only influence came through one son, and
from him, only through daughters. However all seem to agree
that his great attraction was the glorious golden colour of his
coat.

Up to this time the sable, red or brown colouring was disliked by shepherds, being described by them as foxy and frightening to the flocks, but once a dog of this colouring had won in
the show ring, sable collies became popular and were in great
demand. This is possibly the reason why Cockie's service as a
stud dog came later in his life rather than when he was a young-
ster. Of course it is only my opinion, but I do have another
reason for questioning if he had any other significant influence
on the breed. W. Baskerville was a judge and a great authority
on show collies. He was also the breed correspondent for *Our
Dogs*, writing under the name of the 'Collie Chatterer'. He said
that Cockie was bred by a Mr W. White of Nottingham.
According to others he was only shown by Mr White, who
always declined to say where or from whom he purchased the
dog, so that it was without a pedigree. In this case, not
knowing his background, it would not be possible to line-
breed with any success, the coat colouring being the only posi-
tive known factor, and this could have come through from
either of his parents.

W. White was a livestock farmer who also kept kennels at
Bleasby near Southwell, in Nottinghamshire. He contributed
regularly to farming journals and wrote a chapter entitled 'The
Scotch Collie' in *Dogs: Their Points; Whims; Instincts and Peculiarities* (new edition, 1874). The first volume of this booklet
was published in 1870 with Mr Shirley as a regular contributor

on gundogs. In the light of present knowledge about collies Mr White's contribution makes very peculiar reading in places. His illustration of 'Cockie' the Scotch collie would make a perfect example of many of the faults of the modern collie. Endless details are given about the character and show wins of this dog, but nowhere is it stated to whom he belongs, simply that it was a favourite of one of his kennel lads.

Mec, born in 1870, was the property of a Mr John Henshall of Salford, and was also listed as pedigree unknown. He seems to fade out of the scene after a successful show record, and his place was taken by the Irish-bred Shamrock, born in 1870 (Stud Book No. 2897), which is where the known pedigree male line begins. However, it is from his grandson Trefoil, born in 1873 (Stud Book No. 4523), that historians claim all our present-day champions are descended. Trefoil and later his brothers Tartan and Tricolour came from two carefully line-bred litters. The sire was Twig, son of Old Twig, and the dam was Bess, the result of mating great-great-grandson to their maternal great-great-grandmother. The following show reports give us a little more information on Bess and Trefoil.

Report from the FANCIER'S GAZETTE *30 May 1874*

We were so much struck with the superiority of Mr Shirley's dog Trefoil at Northampton show – the only time he has ever been exhibited and where, it will be remembered, he won 1st prize – that we obtained permission to have the portrait drawn from life, which appears with these remarks.

Trefoil is quite a young dog, being now just over 12 months old, and is descended from a very old and pure strain that has been in Mr Shirley's possession for a considerable time.

He is larger than his parents, his sire, Twig, being a small black and tan dog, his dam, Bess, black, tan and white. When a young bitch before she lost her father, a handsomer one it would be hard to find, and also useful to work.

Trefoil himself is a dog of great intelligence and with a most beautiful temperament. We may add that he is worked regularly with a large flock of sheep, and if the time ever comes that prizes are given for combined looks and work in sheep dogs, as for Pointers and Setters, he will prove an opponent of no ordinary pretensions.

It is not strictly correct that he was only exhibited at Northampton, he was shown on at least one other occasion, for in June of that year we have the following report from the Crystal Palace Shows:

Good as the Rough-coated sheepdogs were, Mr Shirley's beautiful black and tan Trefoil stood out in bold relief from the rest, beating even Mr Lacey's Mec and Laddie, that bonnie dog that won at Nottingham and Burton-on-Trent.

Clearly Trefoil caught the eye and had made his mark as a fashionable dog on the show scene. There is no record which states if his show career was terminated in order for him to return to working at Lough Fea, or if he returned to stud at Ettington, but perhaps Mr Shirley's duties in Parliament and also with the new Kennel Club prevented any further exhibiting.

In the course of my investigations I visited Lough Fea and in a corner of the old-world garden behind this magnificent mansion is a dog's graveyard, where I searched in vain among the headstones for the names of some of Mr Shirley's famous collies. As mostly gundogs were buried there I think the herding dogs or collies must have their graves near the home farm.

Another tribute to Mr Shirley's influence on the canine world comes from an issue of the *Stock Keeper*, July 1886. 'Nearly every winning collie of the hour traces its pedigree back to Trefoil, the pick of Mr Shirley's famous strain.'

On the female line, Bess who produced Trefoil in 1873, and Maude who produced Charlemagne in 1879 when mated to Trefoil, were the most influential bitches. A bitch named Wolf owned by a Mr Shaw of Cirencester was a winner at Birmingham in 1872 but nothing more is known about her.

In 1895 the 'improved' collies became known as the rough-coated and smooth-coated collies, two separate breeds, and later that year were separately classified at shows. Then with the formation of the Collie Club in 1898 a new standard was drawn up. By 1910 several clubs catering for the breed had sprung up, including one for the blue merle. At a conference of collie clubs in London on 18 October that year, the standard was revised once more. In 1924 the Collie Club, the Northern Collie Club and the Blue Merle Club amalgamated to become the British Collie Club, and there are now fifteen other collie clubs in Britain and at least one in almost every country of the world.

In 1966 a rough collie breed council was formed under the chairmanship of Clare Malony of the famous Westcarr's prefix. Its first task was to request all the collie clubs for their suggestions to help clarify the old existing standard. Miss Malony felt that the wording of a breed standard should be so clear that there should be absolutely no possibility of misunderstanding it when translated into other languages; this was the intention of the Kennel Club when the newest breed standards were issued in 1986.

This was quite an undertaking when you realize the number of languages into which the wording had to be translated, and all the more difficult if local idioms of expressions were to be avoided. As one of the representatives for the London Collie Club I attended many meetings and took part in many long discussions before we finally agreed upon the wording for a revised standard which was then submitted to the Kennel Club and approved in 1969, and is the one in use until the present day. The breed standard issued by the Collie Club of America differs very slightly from ours, but the British Standard is the one used in all European countries.

Today this breed is one of the most popular show and com-

31 English and Australian Ch. Corydon Handsome Hero, a rough-coated show collie, bred by Mr and Mrs Blake (England) and owned by Mr and Mrs Cake (Australia). *Photo*: Diane Pearce

panion dogs worldwide with registrations increasing each year, and there are many excellent books on the breed, and the numerous clubs catering for it produce newsletters and annual handbooks, besides giving information on the show collies and the progress of the breed.

17

The Smooth-coated Show Collie

The breed is descended from true pastoral dogs, capable of a diversity of tasks, but because smooths have always been the willing slaves of peasants, serfs or men of the road they have not claimed the same literary attention as has been given to the nobleman's dog, and today they are somewhat overshadowed by their own glamorous rough-coated cousins. Unfortunately over the years so much of the blood of the rough-coated 'improved' variety has been introduced into their veins, that with the exception of the coat, their conformation is similar, particularly in head properties. However, the character of a pure smooth is different.

The gene for producing a smooth-coated dog is dominant in most of our herding breeds, and among country folk it is referred to as a 'bare-skinned' dog, with the original sense of 'bear-skinned', black or brown, harsh, dense and completely waterproof.

There are approximately the same number of hairs, inch for inch, on a smooth-coated collie as on a rough, but as both the woolly undercoat and outer harsh-textured coat of the smooth contains more oil, similar to the preening oils of a bird, it is more water-resistant and less likely to hold mud and snow, and the short length of hair lessens the possibility of getting tangled up in briars or undergrowth.

Tracing the history of the smooth-coated pastoral dogs, James Bourchier, as we have already seen, was of the opinion that their ancestors, together with those of the Welsh hillsman and other smooth-coat types, were probably brought to these shores by the goat and sheep herdsmen from North Africa or the Middle East. The Assyrians honoured a dog of similar build on their monuments and described him as 'a graceful animal comely in going'. We are certain the Romans brought from North Africa a type very similar to the smooth-coated collie.

Some North African tribes do not keep dogs at all, on religious grounds, and the Israelites disapproved of dogs, but found them a necessary evil. Most of the dogs of the Middle East are sporting or hunting varieties kept by royal personages purely for pleasure, but for the nomadic peasants, keeping a dog of this nature, where religion allows, can prove very useful.

In most nomadic tribes the animals live as family and become extraordinarily tractable while still retaining their natural instincts, and the herdsmen have wonderful powers over animals, as do members of all primitive tribes. Puppies of Pharoah hounds and other royal sporting dogs often found their way into nomadic family dwellings and readily adapted to this new way of life, many later being crossed with the pariah dog. Indeed the same parallel can be drawn with our own lurchers.

Historians have declared that smooth-coated herding dogs are descended from the gypsies or bandogs, but this assumption is in dispute. Writing about bandogs in 1631, Barnaby Googe gives the following description: 'no gadder abroad, nor lavish with his mouth, barking without cause: neither maketh it any matter though he be not swift, for he is but to fight at home or to give warning of the enimie.' The above description sounds to me like the ideal house dog, and more in keeping with the shepherd's mastiffs, but could indeed also apply to the modern smooth. Other historians claim that the breed is of Scottish origin, but from my researches I am of the opinion that he evolved from dogs first brought to Wales by early settlers, and later brought to Scotland by drovers.

As dogs became more and more accepted as family pets and not just animals for sport or pastoral work, the shepherd's dogs noted for their devotion to their owners became very popular with the ladies of the aristocracy as riding or carriage companions, and as old paintings and photographs will show, the smooth-coated collie was a great favourite, being such an elegant-looking dog and so clean in the drawing rooms. In these circles any form of publicity was considered vulgar, so this variety has never had its share of the limelight.

Queen Victoria favoured the smooth-coated dogs and not the rough-coated, as many believe, and there are the records in Windsor Castle archives to prove this. Several of these smooths presented to her were housed in the kennels at Balmoral. Her favourite collie and constant companion was Sharp, a smooth born in 1854, and who died at the age of fifteen years. Nothing is known of his ancestry, but a statue of him stands over his grave in Windsor Home Park.

One of the most elegant and handsome smooth collies was Noble; he was given to Queen Victoria by Lord Charles Innes-Ker, but bred by Mr Thomas Elliot of Hindhope, a member of a famous shepherding family. Noble became the sire of several royal collies.

Before the purely show variety emerged, many farmers and flockmasters preferred the smooth-coated working dogs and bred true lines of smooth-coated herding dogs for several generations for hill and pasture work and to compete on the trial field. Today many of the top working and trial winners are smooth-coated. As I explained earlier, most of the butchers'

32 Portrait of Noble, a smooth-coated collie given to
Queen Victoria by Lord Charles Innes-Ker, son of the
6th Duke of Roxburghe. Reproduced by gracious
permission of HM The Queen

dogs were similar to the present-day smooth-coated collie.

In 1890 Rawdon B. Lee wrote in his *Collie or Sheepdog*:

At the Trials, the smooth-coated dogs, as a rule, more
nearly approach the show bench form than do their rough-
jacketed cousins, for speed and endurance are required
rather than long woolly coats, huge 'frills' and 'brushes'
big enough to disgrace the best that ever hurry behind the
boldest of bold reynards.

Even today, in the right hands and bred on the right lines, the
show variety is capable of performing almost any herding task
required of him, as I have witnessed, and can still be a graceful
winner in the show ring.

Herding Dogs

In *The Dog Book 1906* James Watson's chapter on smooth sheepdogs is difficult to comprehend, but as the gentleman was an American (albeit of Scottish descent) one shall overlook his ignorance on the subject. However, where he states, 'We cannot compliment a single one of our forerunners in their contribution to the history of sheepdogs in England. Yet there is not in the whole category of dogs of the British Isles a simpler record to unfold,' one wonders how he arrived at that conclusion. In the same chapter he goes on to give accounts of bobtails and curs, finally ending up by giving long descriptions of American smooth champions, scale of breed points, and particulars of conformation, and interspersed with all this we have descriptions of the various methods of working with these dogs, including heelers! Three pages are devoted to lines of poetry about all manner of odd tykes. What, one might ask, has all this got to do with smooth collies? In my opinion it is simply 'padding', but he may be forgiven for most canine books ignore this variety altogether.

The ancestry of some of the original parents of this variety goes far back into history, but the formula for the development of the variety into a fixed registered breed with its own breed standard followed the same pattern as that of the 'improved' rough collies. Today in truth he is only a smooth-coated version of these, with a few subtle differences noted in the wording of the standard, yet very different in character. There is no separate standard for him issued by the American Collie Club, just a paragraph about the coat difference.

Until specialist breeding for coat texture became popular, smooth- and rough-coated puppies could appear in some litters in all varieties of herding dogs, and still do to a lesser extent, as in the natural order of things the genes for a smooth coat are dominant over those for rough.

In America today the roughs and smooths are so interbred

that both are virtually the same breed but wearing a different length of overcoat, and in fact as I have said it is considered unnecessary to issue a separate breed standard as we do here in the UK, where he is more selectively bred from dominant smooth parents. However, correct coat and conformation are still the prime objective of the breeders, while other hereditary factors or instincts are completely ignored through lack of opportunity to display them.

The first separate classification for the smooth-coated sheepdogs in the show ring was at Darlington in 1870; there were fifteen entries and among these were smooth-coated bobtails. Apparently, no prizes were awarded and frankly, I am not surprised. More information on this is given in the chapter on tailless stock dogs.

The first smooth-coated collie to win in a separate class for the breed was Mr Darbell's Nett in 1872, but no further details are given. The first entry for a smooth-coated collie in the Kennel Club Stud Book was Scott 2895, by Shep out of Bess and belonging to Messrs Bancroft and Taylor of Rawtenstall in Lancashire. Many of the early champion show winners came from around this district, one of the most famous being the Laund Kennels owned by the late Mr W. W. Stansfield. His daughter Ada Bishop still owns the kennels and continues to breed the famous Laund collies. Mrs Hill of the Selskars prefix bred many good smooths which are in the pedigrees of several winning in the ring today.

In 1874 a Mr W. W. Thompson won first prize with two smooth bitches in Nottingham Dog Show, but I can find no other details. Before 1877 several of the bigger shows provided classes for smooths, and at the Birmingham National Show that year Mr Mapplebeck's blue merle Fan was awarded first prize, with Mr W. W. Thompson's tricolour Yarrow second, and Mr T. B. Swinburn's tricolour Lassie in third place. All three gentlemen owned very successful breed kennels, but the title of 'father of the breed' went to Mr Alex Hastie whose 'Herdwich' prefix became famous.

Mr Theo Marples, editor of *Our Dogs*, and Mr Mumford Smith were other famous early names, the former owning Ch. Melody, one of the first smooth champions, and the latter having bred the famous champions Eleanor de Montford and Julian de Montford.

By the turn of the century some very smart, excellent-quality smooths were gracing the show ring and frequently gained high honours warding off the challenge of their rough-coated cousins. Today the breed is mainly in the hands of a few dedicated breeders or exhibitors who because they keep one or more 'retired oldies' in the house or kennel, have to accept severe restrictions when retaining any young stock for future shows, mostly due to domestic situations and the limitations on selling surplus puppies. All of us hope our geese will turn into swans, but we are often forced to sell off our promising cygnets before we can await the future results from our planned meetings.

The Collie Club founded in 1881 with Mr Shirley at its head catered for both coats. The Club was reformed in 1886. The first Smooth Collie Club was formed in 1898. In 1895 a combined rough and smooth standard and scale of points for judging was issued. It differed from the smooth only in coat requirement, which laid down that the coat should be short, dense and flat, with a good texture and an abundance of undercoat.

The present Smooth Collie Club of Great Britain was founded in 1955 and its very hardworking committee has done much to further the interests of the breed. The Club submitted a separate breed standard to the Kennel Club in 1966.

In 1972 the Kennel Club drafted a proposal to forbid the interbreeding between rough and smooth varieties after 1976, bearing in mind that by that time the breeds would have

33 Ch. Tilehouse Patrick, a modern smooth-coated show
collie bred and owned by the author. *Photo*: G. B.
Royffé

separate standards, and asked the Club to study this proposal.
After much discussion the Club pointed out to the Kennel Club
that as yet the breed did not have sufficient stud dogs of un-
related bloodlines and therefore they could not agree to such a
proposal, so as a result it was dropped by the Kennel Club.

In 1973 the Kennel Club sent a copy of their proposed
separate smooth collie standard to the Club for their com-
ments. In essence this differed little from the rough standard.
After much discussion, with the exception of some slight
changes of wording, the Club decided to accept the Kennel
Club's proposed standard and it was given full approval in

1974. For a time the two record-winning post-war smooths to gain the biggest number of CCs were Ch. Selskar's Soldanora bred by Mrs Hill and owned by Mr and Mrs Saville, and my own Ch. Tilehouse Patrick. Neither, however, figures as a key dog in the breed, an honour that would probably go to a dog from the Peterblue Kennels, although more recently there have been several smooths who have equalled or beaten this record. However, their story belongs to more modern times.

At the present time there is no specialist book on the breed, only a chapter or two included in books on the rough collie. The breed has not been glamorized to the same extent as the 'Lassies' and therefore has a smaller following. Perhaps one day the fashion will change and one of our most ancient breeds will earn its rightful place in the popularity poll.

There is one specialist club always able and willing to help and advise, but a few of the Rough Collie Clubs also take the smooth under their wing.

18

The White Collie

In the USA the white collie, both rough- and smooth-coated, has a great many admirers. There is a club devoted to the variety, and a separate register and breed standard approved by the American Kennel Club, and they are also separately classified at shows, but it is not a true breed, simply a colour variety of the show collie, which fashion and finance have gone hand in hand to popularize.

White collies are not recognized by the English Kennel Club and in fact some collie breed standards state that predominantly white dogs are undesirable. The only reason I include them in this study is because they originated in Britain, and the history of their emergence gives a good indication of how lines in collies were exploited for commercial gain.

In the shepherding world today an all-white sheepdog or collie is not favoured. Many shepherds feel that sheep do not fear or respect a white or almost white dog. Others on the other hand argue that a good dog can hold its sheep no matter what its colour, and long ago shepherds kept white, partly white or blue merle herding dogs for their value around the lambing pens, as it was felt they had a less disturbing effect on the young lambs.

Zoologically speaking, white animals are supposed to be

Herding Dogs

stronger and more aggressive. In experiments it has been found that when crossing albinos with normal colours, each generation became more aggressive as it became whiter. In one particular experiment with mice, the new race eventually died out, by killing each other off.

White is the basic body colour of collies, with a blanket of some other colour, usually black, thrown over. This can also be brown, with a variation or combination of each plus the usual white markings to a greater or lesser degree, on chest, legs, feet and tip of tail and often a blaze on muzzle and head. Those which have a predominance of white on the body and legs are known as 'white-factored'. This means that the dog has a completely unbroken white strip from under the chin, along the belly and down the outside of the hind legs to the feet, and sometimes along the underside of the tail as well. If the white is only on the inside of hind legs, it is not a white factoring.

Mating two white-factored collies together can produce a white or mostly white pup in the litter and these pups will be perfectly normal in every way, but mating two blue merles together can produce a white pup which is almost always abnormal, being either blind or deaf, or both, and in severe cases having no eyes at all. These pups are sometimes referred to as albinos, a recessive homogeneous gene which lacks pigment, but the term is not strictly correct in this case.

For this reason the American white collie breed standard states that merle markings on a white collie are undesirable. The American white show collies are very attractive and usually have black or sable colourings on the ears and sometimes a small patch on the rump, and possess good temperaments.

The all-white collie first came into prominence through Queen Victoria's children. I feel there must have been times during the early part of Victoria's reign when the royal kennels at Windsor or Balmoral could have been compared to the

Battersea Dogs' Home! Whenever the royal children stopped to admire a dog or a puppy of any breed, within the next few months a number of pups of that breed would arrive at one of the royal residence as gifts for the children, and these received great publicity in the local press.

The following extract is from Hugh Dalziel's *The Collie: Its History, Points and Breeding*:

> I am not advocating the breeding of collies of any special, peculiar or unusual colours, but white ones may possibly soon become the rage, from the fact that the Queen and His Royal Highness the Prince of Wales, having each graciously accepted a white collie from those noted breeders Messrs J. & W. H. Charles of Wellesbourne, Warwickshire, their sire being the Charles' well known dog 'The Squire', who as well as their dam, is of the most fashionable pedigree.

Mr D. J. Thompson Gray of Dundee owns a collie all white with the exception of a spot near the root of her tail. Mr Witley of Lynn possesses two he bred that are white with the exception of the ears, which are a fawn colour; all of these are pure bred.

Hugh Dalziel deduced:

> From these facts, and as doubtless there are many other cases of white collies that have not come under my notice, it will be seen that the establishment of a strain of white collies is not impossible. Whether it is desirable to do so is, of course, a matter of opinion; but if collies are to be treated as dogs of the fancy there can be no objection to the multiplication of varieties distinguished by colours. If there is a demand for these it is to be feared that crosses from the Spitz dog will be palmed off on the unwary as pure bred.

We now know that is exactly what did happen. A strain of

white collies was established and some odd crosses were palmed off on the unwary. The all-white collie never found much favour with English exhibitors, yet it became a fashionable drawing room pet and one was presented to Princess Beatrice as a wedding present in July 1885.

According to Mr McGlynn, a representative for an American canine journal, the American breeders were more progressive than the conservative British, but were not very careful from whom or where they obtained their original stock. He states that 'genetics was then an unproved science, and some promoters/breeders allegedly used a Samoyed cross to get the desired white coat thus producing an all white collie.'

Others have suggested a cross with the borzoi, and Mr Southwell, who was in charge of the borzois at the kennels, told me that white collies were born at Sandringham kennels as a result of crossing show collies with Queen Alexandra's famous borzois. He said they were gentle, beautiful creatures, but usually from the wrong side of the blanket, as he put it! He also told me that quite a number of the pups from the crossings were bought by the big commercial kennels of the day and it was from these offspring that the longer, leaner head of the modern collie emerged.

The waning popularity of the colour was given another boost in 1887 when a white with a tricoloured head won a first prize at Glamis show, which was attended by royalty. Its name is given as Scottish Fancier, but I feel this may only have been an odd way of describing its owner.

This win, plus the royal patronage, caught the imagination of American fanciers, but it was a letter to the dog press from an American journalist which gave the strain its biggest boost. It read as follows:

> There is a considerable demand in this country for all white
> collies and it seems possible that blue/merle breeders in

England who at times get these 'misfits' as a result of too
closely following colour lines, ought to put themselves in
touch with buyers through our columns. Better to spend a
few dollars in this way than to bucket the unwelcome ones.
One breeder who owns a white stud tells us that his dog
sired eleven all white pups from the last twenty puppies
born to him. There is no accounting for taste, but it would
appear to be their business to drown puppies in England
which are wanted in America . . .

Such an advertisement today would result in a howl of pro-
tests, but soon after it appeared, white puppies and a stud dog
that could produce whites were being offered in all the canine
journals, and an example of one such offer is reproduced here.
The Southport Kennels in Liverpool were known to have produced several white collies, but most of these seem to have been
from blue matings. In fact Southport White Squaw, born in
1908, was actually advertised as invaluable for merle produc-
tion, even though she was overshot or pig-jawed as they
described it. May she perhaps have been deaf and blind as well?

She was by two blue merles, Blue John and Strawberry Girl.
Blue John was exported to Thomas Daws of Hartford, USA,
and used a great deal at stud out there. This kennel certainly believed in advertising their goods, as at one time they claimed
that champion Southport Sample was the champion collie of
the world!

The ancestry of most of the good whites in the USA goes
back to the British bitch, the Lily, born in 1880, and sired by
Trevor out of Hasty of Carlisle. Both sire and dam went back
to the famous Trefoil.

The first modern white to gain the title of champion was Ch.
Sterling Silver Flash in 1939. She appears to have been an all-
American-bred bitch. The photo of the white collie champion I
have chosen as a present-day representative of the breed, is

Edith Levine's Ch. Glen Knolls Flash Lightning, a sable-headed white. Not only have I seen and examined this striking dog, but it is interesting that at the time I saw him he had already sired five champions, one white, two sable/white and two tricolours.

There are a few smooth-coated white collies, but those I have seen have not impressed me greatly as they appeared to have large colour patches on the body.

At the turn of the century serious breeders were concerned at the number of collies born either deaf or partially deaf, and also becoming blind at an early age. The deafness could be traced back to certain lines which were known to have produced white pups, but some breeders held the opinion that the blindness came from lines known to have been crossed with setters.

In those days it was difficult to prove that any defects were of an hereditary nature, but when the breed standard was changed at a meeting of collie clubs in 1910 it was decided to include a colour section reading 'all white or red setter colouring is most objectionable'. This was indeed a diplomatic move and breeders were satisfied to leave the white fancy to their friends across the Big Pond.

For centuries herding dogs have been bred from the survival of the fittest, no matter what their colour. Once man has interfered with the rules of nature, then all sorts of health and temperament problems begin to emerge. Probably the saddest influence is the health damage done to a breed when these natural gene patterns are interfered with by crossing with another breed to achieve some fashionable feature.

Fortunately the great strides in the field of medicine and genetics have helped us to overcome a great many of these problems and today it can be truly said that the white collie is not only an established variety of collie, but is as sound mentally and physically as any of the other colours, and the specialist breeders make every effort to keep it that way.

This interesting extract from *The Ladies' Kennel Journal,* March 1896, entitled 'Bow-Wow' by Betty Barkis, was kindly sent to me by Clarice Waud:

> I am glad to hear that white collies are to become popular, for it is certainly a very beautiful variety of a very beautiful breed. Shepherds, so I have read somewhere, dislike white collies, as they say that the lambs mistake them for some exceptionally attractive sort of sheep and follow them about. Which, if true, goes to prove that lambs have a sense of colour.
>
> The white collie, Cambridge Surprise, who was first in his class at Crufts, was claimed at the catalogue price, namely £10, by Lady Aylesford, Miss M. Garnett, Mr Panmure-Gordon, and some others, all hoping to have become possessed of such a decided bargain. However, the Kennel Club Show rule that, when more than one claimant appears the dog is to be sold by auction, was carried out; and, accordingly, 12.30 on a Friday in March 1896 was named for the sale. No auctioneer was forthcoming, so the intending buyers were kept waiting for nearly two hours; and, when the auctioneer arrived only two purchasers put in an appearance, Miss M. Garnett and Mr Panmure-Gordon. When Miss Garnett's bid of £30 was quickly followed by Mr Panmure-Gordon's guineas, she was heard to remark 'Only two buyers! I shall not bid against Mr Gordon.' So that lucky gentleman got the coveted prize at a lower figure than he expected, although he made no secret of his determination to possess the animal, even if it ran up to £100!

I have not yet been able to trace anything about the breeding of Cambridge Surprise, but Mr Panmure-Gordon, who was President of the Scottish Kennel Club, was so pleased with him that he commissioned Maud Earl, the talented and fashionable English canine artist, to paint this dog together with one of his favourite black-and-tan collies.

34 Maud Earl, RA, *Two Collies*. The dogs were owned by
Mr Panmure-Gordon, a President of the Scottish
Kennel Club. The white collie is believed to be Cam-
bridge Surprise. *Photo*: Sotheby's

A few years ago in Sotheby's sale catalogue I saw that a
picture of two collies by Maud Earl belonging to the late Mr
Panmure-Gordon was for sale. I went to London for the view
day and discovered that the painting was probably the one of
Cambridge Surprise. On enquiring if it was likely to fetch a
price within the limits I could afford, I was told that the works
of Maud Earl were fetching big prices at that time. I came home
disappointed, having left a tentative bid with the auctioneers,
and was later informed that this was not sufficient, and that the
painting had been bought by the family firm of Panmure-
Gordon & Co. of London, who have kindly given me permission to reproduce it here.

Another famous painting of a white collie which hangs in the

35   Ch. Glen Knolls Flash Lightning, a modern white
collie, bred and owned by Mrs Daniel Levine (USA)

White House in Washington, D.C., is that Rob Roy seated
beside Mrs Grace Goodhue Coolidge with a view of the house
in the background. Influential owners or sudden changes of
fashion can have a pronounced effect on the popularity of a
breed or variety.

19

The Border Collie

36 Claud Carion, *The Farmyard* (1894), showing border collie pups of almost 100 years ago. *Photo*: Maxwell-Hyslop

The border collie is a pearl of great price; he has been cultured and developed from the best strains of our ancient British herding dogs mentioned in the previous chapter. This makes him a highly versatile performer in almost any role, but it is as a sheepdog that he has earned world renown.

In my book *Border Collies*, published in 1978, I have discussed almost every aspect of the breed, including its full history, so here I propose only to deal with the history of his emergence from a variety of working sheepdog to a pure fixed breed in its own right.

First, a few details of how the pure fixed breed got its name. With the formation of the International Sheepdog Society in 1906 the clasp was added to a valuable pearl necklace which by now encircled the whole shepherding world. In the Society's stud book, instituted in 1955, all shepherd's dogs were registered only as working sheepdogs, rough, smooth or bearded, yet in the Society's literature they were referred to as border collies, as indeed were those which went overseas, with the exception of those registered as beardies.

Some years later the words border collie were added in parenthesis on the ISDS registration certificate, a name that Mr Reid, the first secretary of the Society, had given to this new recognized pure breed of sheepdog, but it was not until 1976 that the breed was officially recognized and registered at the Kennel Club as border collie, and put on the canine map with an approved breed standard. This was issued through the efforts of a newly formed specialized breed club, the Border Collie Club of Great Britain.

In the past almost any black or brown dog with four white feet and a tip to its tail was labelled as a sheepdog or collie. Some bit, some barked, others herded or hunted and all commanded varying degrees of human respect, but the shepherds or flockmasters on the big sheep runs of the border counties between England and Scotland had developed a strain of sheepdog which worked in a unique manner; known generally as the 'eye dog' and kept pure for generations, as I have explained earlier, he was probably descended from the old forest dogs for the build and method of working are too similar to be ignored.

At the beginning of this century, with an increasing population and increasing affluence, the buyers of both flesh and fleece required animals in the best possible condition to meet higher demands. Having produced a better animal to meet the demands of the market it was now necessary to own a suitable flock dog to manage them. Border collie types working low to the ground and using the power of the eye to control the flock, proved better suited and caused less injury to the stock than the old strong pushing types. In addition they excelled at the sheepdog trials which were the public platform for testing their skills.

The reason Mr Reid gave this type of working sheepdog the name border collie, was because the best strains came from the Border counties and, being a Scotsman, he would obviously add the term collie, not sheepdog, thus distinguishing it from other herding types.

Since the dog was bred only for its performance, not its conformation, it was not felt necessary to issue a breed standard, but the scene soon changed. The intelligence and distinctive method of working of these dogs caught the imagination of the public as well as of shepherds in other countries, and owners soon found a new and lucrative market for any surplus puppies.

After the Second World War the craze for obedience and working trial competitions started, and border collies proved very efficient in this role too, but as these competitions were run under Kennel Club rules the question of registration arose with this particular body. Meetings between the Kennel Club and the ISDS were convened to discuss the matter. Captain Whittaker, chairman of the ISDS at the time, took the chair at the first meeting, and Mr Dunn, the secretary, represented the

The Border Collie

Society. Mr Wilson Stephens, the press reporter and editor of *The Field*, was one of the Kennel Club representatives; in all, a very worthy gathering.

The furthermost point upon which agreement was reached regarding the status of these dogs was in 1960, when the Kennel Club agreed that they would only describe as border collie dogs already registered in the stud book of the ISDS and these would only be accepted for entry in the obedience register, otherwise they were to appear on the Kennel Club register only as working collies or sheepdogs. At this point, however, the ISDS only recognized and registered these dogs as working sheep-dogs.

There was still considerable opposition even to this decision, but Captain Whittaker and the ISDS directors agreed that this was a splendid arrangement in the circumstances, and an indication of good relations with the Kennel Club. The arrangement later caused much anger and confusion among owners of border collies in the obedience world. Many so-called border collies with impressive pedigrees and sold by farmers were not ISDS-registered, and therefore could only be accepted on the Kennel Club register as working collies or sheepdogs, even if they were never likely to see a sheep. The reluctance of farmers to register their litter is threefold. Firstly they had to be members of the ISDS and this was an expense not warranted in their opinion unless they wished to compete in sheepdog trials run under Society rules. Secondly, litters could only be regis-tered if a mating card had been signed and returned to the society within a limited time of mating. Filling in forms unless absolutely essential or a government requirement is not the strong point of any farmer, and in many cases farmers were not even aware a mating had taken place. Thirdly, they argued that registration with any governing body did nothing to improve working ability of their dogs.

To avoid the possibility of losing some very good working

Herding Dogs

strain through lack of a registration number, there was, however, a clause in the ISDS constitution which allowed collies to be registered 'on merit' after completing a working test, but the clause carried the words 'provided the Sire and Dam is registered Rule 4(s)' which almost nullified the point, although it seems to have been overcome in a few cases.

In 1961 the ISDS Council decided to amend this rule to allow a non-pedigree dog to become registered 'on merit' provided something was known about its breeding. At one time, to save wasted journeys, provision was made for inspection of a dog's work on the home farm, before going for a test of merit. It was due to this new rule, or amendment to the rule, that I first became acquainted with Mr Dunn, the secretary of the Society at that time, as I had the audacity to apply to register one of my working collies in this way.

When the Kennel Club Obedience Council was formed they set to work to try to clarify the registration problem once more. Then in 1963 the Australian Kennel Council approved and adopted a border collie breed standard, which had previously been approved by several individual states in Australia, and Challenge Certificates were also on offer.

Those of us who had the privilege of going to Australia to judge other collie breeds found ourselves sometimes being required to judge border collies to an Australian breed standard where none existed in the country of origin at that time; in fact the breed was not even eligible to be shown under Kennel Club rules, except in the obedience ring.

Added to this, border collies imported from Britain were being exhibited on the Continent and required to be judged to an Australian standard, in fact, the only breed standard. Clearly this situation could not continue, but the ISDS directors still persisted in an ostrich attitude to the matter, since their concern with these dogs was only in a working capacity.

Major Harry Glover, a well-known international dog judge,

who sat on several committees of the Kennel Club, decided to take the matter into his own hands and to press for action, and helped to form the Border Collie Club of Great Britain, founded in 1975, and originally called the British Border Collie Club.

The Kennel Club can only act if an application for recognition is put forward, together with a proposed breed standard, by a specialist club, and in this case the one submitted by the new Club was based on the Australian standard. Many felt that the first standard should have been submitted by the ISDS, but they insisted that dogs entered in their stud book were still regarded as working sheepdogs, and only their performance in that capacity was recorded, or in fact their concern. This was a very valid point and had to be respected, so it was back to the drawing board once more.

A record of further developments is best summarized in a report from the former secretary of the ISDS, Lance Alderson, who was present at all subsequent meetings and for which I have the chairman's permission to quote here.

INTERNATIONAL SHEEP DOG SOCIETY
St Andrew's House
Haughton Road
Darlington

June 1976

Foreword by Secretary

By the time this newsletter reaches you, there is every probability that the Border Collie will have been recognized by the Kennel Club as a breed for show purposes. Despite the various approaches from the Society, and despite all the letters, petitions, and appeals made direct from the Members to the Kennel Club

hierarchy to disregard applications for recognition of the
breed, the pressure on the Kennel Club from those who
hold the contrary view that the Border Collie should be
shown has apparently been irresistible, and 'recognition' is
imminent. The Society is grateful to all members and
others who have taken up cudgels on behalf of the Border
Collie, and I am truly sorry that I have not better news to
report.

From a meeting with Kennel Club officer-holders (of
whom, you will be interested to learn, several were
completely against 'recognition' for the correct reason that
the Border Collie is a working dog, inappropriate to the
show bench, but they had to consider the requests of
others quite impartially) it appears that the principal cause
of their concern is that whether a recognized breed or not,
Border Collie shows are being planned, and if these are
held outside the jurisdiction of the Kennel Club or other
authoritative body (like the ISDS), there is a grave danger
that discipline and organization would be lacking, and
there would be an even greater danger that entries might
not be properly checked and authenticated, thereby
opening the door for any old thing which looks reasonably
near to be presented as a Border Collie. If/when they
become involved in Border Collie shows, it is the intention
of the Kennel Club to use the ISDS Stud Book records –
they have purchased them for many years – and anything
which is not descended from ISDS registered stock, and
fully traceable, will not be accepted in the show class, on
similar lines to the rules applied by the KC for 'working
sheepdogs' in their obedience classes.

Whilst the spirit of the very word 'show' is abhorrent to
the majority of the Society membership, and you may
consider that by implication, above, the ISDS might be the
authoritative body governing Border Collie shows to be

out of place, I must remind you that our Constitution document is quite clear in this context. Read page 3 paragraph 2(a), but in case that small grey booklet eludes you, this is what it says:

First, the preamble under the heading of 'OBJECTS' reads (briefly) 'The main object of the Society shall be to promote and foster within and throughout the United Kingdom and such other countries as may seem desirable or necessary, the breeding, training, and improvement in the interests and for the welfare or benefit of the community, of the breeds and strains of sheep dogs, to secure the better management of stock by improving the shepherd's dog, and to achieve such main object by such means as the Society may from time to time determine, and in particular (but without limitation on the generality of the foregoing) by: . . . and here we come to para. (a)

> *'The promotion or organisation of Sheep Dog Trials,*
> *Exhibitions or Shows, with competitive or non-*
> *competitive, and either in association or unassociated*
> *with any other societies, bodies, or persons, like or*
> *suitable occasions or events.'*

I have underlined 'sheep dog trials', which we all know about, but it is not abundantly clear what was actually meant by the words, also underlined, 'exhibitions or shows', when the Constitution was adopted and became Society law.

Disregarding the 'exhibitions', the 'show' elements come in for scrutiny. Constitution permits them, yet very few seem to want them, and furthermore are very indignant when anyone else steps in, and with the advent of the British Border Collie Club, which I understand is now well and truly 'off the ground', whose sole purpose and reasons for existence is, I understand, to develop the Border Collie and to show it competitively, it would probably be timely to amend our Constitution and completely eradicate the 'show' part of the Objects in view of our attitude towards showing. Either that, or we should assert our right to be the authoritative body governing the showing of the Border Collie, and I have little doubt that the Kennel Club would welcome the co-operation of those whom they regard as the experts – quite rightly – on the Border Collie.

The one main concept of 'showing' which annoys and upsets most Members is the fact that a 'standard' will have to be adopted for breeders to breed to and judges to judge to, with what diabolical result is hard to envisage, but it is quite evident that, as has already been forecast in the canine press, there will henceforth be two sorts of Border Collie, those which look pretty and earn their keep on the show bench, and those which are just as handsome but maybe vary in size, coat, etc. and earn their daily bread by hard work on the farm or moorland stray and occasionally compete in sheep dog trials, or alternatively those which have no stock to tend but are kept for obedience work. No matter what, the Society will probably still register or record some 5000+ pups per year, destined for work in some form or other, but how many will be groomed for stardom on the show bench? Your guess is as good as mine, but you can be assured that it will be a very tiny percentage of the total number of dogs employed in honest-to-goodness work. For this reason, I find it very difficult to accept the allegation that 'recognition will completely ruin the breed'. It will most certainly ruin the few that find their way into this unnatural situation, but this need not affect your herding dog, nor need it affect my obedience dog if we do not wish it so to do.

I cannot foresee any shepherd or any farmer, or for that matter, any obedience exponent, taking their brood bitch to a show champion Border Collie for service – at least, not in the sincere hope of getting a litter of potential workers. Conversely, however, it may well be that in the initial stages at least, that those with breeding to a standard in mind will seek the use of one or other of the many very handsome Trials dogs available at the present time. Eventually, though, they too will have their own breeding lines, and the partition of the two sorts of collie will be complete. Reluctant as I am to say it, I am afraid that this is inevitable.

I am not suggesting for one moment that if we ignore this, it will go away, but must add some support to the recent writings of one of our obedience trials Members who felt that the Society had lost the battle before it began. Let us not be too despondent about it, these 'fads' have been known to die before this.

It is only right to acknowledge that every day in the office we have growing proof that there is a very great deal of keen interest in the Border Collie as a pet dog. I take an average of four phone calls per day from people enquiring where they can purchase one, preferably not from a working strain, and one lady was rather upset when I denied knowing from where she could obtain one which would fit in with the breed standard. Last year at this time similar enquiries were occurring about three times per week, so it appears that the 'fashion' is catching on quite rapidly but it does not essentially follow that all are destined for the show bench, as 'One Man and His Dog' has brought it home to many of the uninitiated what a beautiful dog the Border Collie is.

It is none the less alarming to realize that there must now be many enthusiasts eagerly awaiting publication of a breed standard so that they may jump on the show Border Collie bandwagon to breed them right, left and centre until they get something which might closely resemble a Border Collie, conforming to a standard, and doing the damage that all have feared from the very inception of the idea, but the breeder-members of the Society, and only they, can ensure that this damage is confined to those on the bench, and is not allowed to infiltrate into the 'working-classes' of Border Collie.

Obviously all we can do now is to sit back and watch what happens next, but whilst it is happening you folk who own the genuine article will continue to breed them, buy them, sell them, register them, train them, work them, trial them, and at the end of the day, when the show fad has either died out or has assumed its true perspective, you'll still emerge unscathed by it all.

These were stern words but we now know the fad has not faded out. In fact the breed has become a very popular show dog and gives a lot of pleasure to those who admire it but do not have the facilities to use it for farm work, but I will always think that as mentioned in Lance Alderson's report on the ISDS, not to take full control and acknowledge this type of collie as a pure fixed breed was an opportunity lost.

In 1979 the Southern Border Collie Club was formed and soon afterwards the Kennel Club invited representatives of the ISDS and both breed clubs to a meeting in London for further discussions on the breed standard and other points before granting the breed Championship status.

In order that the title of Champion gained by a dog in the show ring should not be confused with or detract from the title of National or Supreme International Champion, a title gained by a dog for its performance in the field, the representatives present agreed that a border collie winning three CCs under Kennel Club rules should only be entitled to be called a Show Champion, unless it could prove its worth as a sheep worker.

All present agreed upon a format for such a test, and to be judged by two judges appointed by the ISDS in the presence of both secretaries. The Kennel Club has also made provision in its rules for a dog to be tested on cattle, should it be requested.

Following this meeting an amended breed standard was approved by the Kennel Club in November 1980, and Challenge Certificates were first on offer to the breed at Crufts 1982. It was sad that the judge appointed to award the first set of CCs, the late Major Henry Glover, who had done so much to put the breed on the canine map, could not officiate through illness. His place was taken by Mrs C. Sutton, a very experienced international 'all-rounder', who awarded the first dog CC to my Tilehouse Cassius of Beagold, owned by Joyce Collis and Felix Cosme who handled the dog throughout his successful show career. (I give more details about the dog later.) The first bitch CC went to Eric Broadhurst's Tracelyn Gal bred by Mr J. Ritchie. She is by Cyrmo out of Jill. Both the CC winners became Show Champions later.

It is sad that so little is known about Maid, the first entry in the ISDS stud book. It is even claimed by the family of her late breeder that the photograph in the stud book purporting to be her is in fact one of an old farm pup which may have been submitted in error, or possibly it was the only photograph available which was suitable for reproduction. Not a great deal is known either about the first ISDS Sheepdog Champion, so let us not fail to record details of the early show winners before all is forgotten.

There are several books recording the achievements of early trials winners, or border collies making their mark in shepherding history, but here is a record of the early achievements in the show ring, which belongs to canine history, and which may be of great interest to future generations of fanciers of the breed, together with some interesting background details leading up to the crowning of the first dog and bitch border

37   A modern border collie at work. *Photo*: Marc Henrie

collie Show Champions.

The first dog and bitch Show Champions were crowned on the same day, 16 July 1982, at the National Working Breeds Championship Show held at Malvern. The judge was Mr Bill Finlay, a Scotsman who has a practical knowledge of the border collie as a shepherd's dog, trial dog and show exhibit. I will first give some background history of the dog, not because I bred him, but because like twins, one has to come first, and in the canine world, the dog gets this privilege.

Having been opposed to the idea of border collies becoming show dogs, I suddenly became aware that such a move was inevitable, and switched sides only in the hope that I could in some way help to preserve some of the breed's distinctive qualities and somehow combine good looks with working qualities, through careful selection. A philosophy to which I have always subscribed is 'If you can't beat 'em, join 'em', but it was the knowledge that a clear breed standard would be forthcoming from this move that really swayed me – but how I wish it could have been put forward by the ISDS, the real authorities on these dogs.

Years of attending sheepdog sales and trials, hours of studying lines and pedigrees gave me a good idea of the lines I wanted to combine in any future breeding programme. By this time I needed to buy new and International Sheep Dog-registered stock, as my own dogs were pedigree but unregistered, a fact which was now assuming more importance than the quality of their work.

I made my plans known to Barbara Houseman, the first lady to be appointed to the Council of the ISDS, who told me that Will and Barbara Carpenter bred exactly the lines I wanted and had a litter at the time, although she doubted they would allow me to have a puppy for my purpose.

In fear and trepidation I visited the Carpenters' farm in Gloucestershire. Their hospitality and the welcome from the dogs was overwhelming, but Will was very much against allowing me to have a pup. Fortunately Barbara, who had been giving serious thought to this new situation in the sheepdog circle, also shared my view, and after much heart-searching on all sides, I was allowed to have the pup of my choice, the tricolour Brocken Sweep. I added my Tilehouse prefix when he was Kennel Club-registered, Brocken being the Carpenters' prefix, and Barbara and her late husband Will competed in trials and bred some very fine border collies, which Barbara continues to do.

Sweep's temperament was superb and his physical appearance was, in my opinion, near perfection. The hunt was then on for a bitch of equal merits. Barbara Carpenter located the sweet, winning, black-and-white little Fly, bred by George Lloyd from good trial-winning stock, and persuaded him to sell her to me.

On paper, the combination of the lines seemed perfect, and their physical appearance seemed to complement. It only remained for me to test my plans and theories with the progeny from a litter, and this soon arrived.

Tilehouse Cassius was one of that resulting litter, but of the six pups there were three others which, if given the same treatment and advantages as Cassius, could also have become Champions. I felt I had proved my point, but domestic circumstances prevented me from attending shows at that time and I sold Cassius to Joyce Collis. She bought the pup for her partner, Felix Cosme, as a birthday present, and later they added the 'Beagold' prefix to his name.

The first bitch Show Champion, and one of equal importance, is a lovely black-and-white collie that has all the attributes of the breed and also comes from good working stock. Show Champion Muirend Border Dream, together with her sporting and sympathetic owner/breeder Nan Simpson, has travelled thousands of miles from their Scottish home to grace the show-rings.

She is by Pioneer of Muirend. He too had all the qualities one looks for in a border collie. Unfortunately, after siring two or three litters, he met with an accident at a friend's farm where he was working, and had to be put down, but Nan Simpson did breed Muirend Border Reiver from him. He is the sire of a lot of winning stock today and a half-brother to Border Dream, both being by Pioneer.

The dam was registered as Nimble of Muirend. She was also a working bitch – not a big one – but could jump anything, hence her name. There were four puppies in the litter, two dogs and two bitches. Muirhead Border Dream was one of them: Mrs Simpson says that she has never been let down in giving her that name, and that she is a lovely-natured bitch, very easy to train and always wanting to please.

A third border collie to gain his title in 1982 was Asoka Navajho of Firelynx, and his is something of a hard luck story, for he had made all the running in the early shows right up to the final furlong of the Champion stakes. This very handsome, strongly built, black-and-white dog is a different type from Cassius, whilst equally conforming to the breed standard. He was the first exhibit to make a great impression on the show scene and was best of breed almost every time he was shown. When the two dogs had to challenge for CCs Cassius would pull out all the stops and co-operate to please his owner, whilst Buck (as he is known at home) would look at his owner as if to say, 'I've done my bit for the breed, let him have it this time!'

Finally, with a new coat and renewed vigour, he decided that as his mistress was trying her hand with another breed at shows, he would keep up the honour of Firelynx by gaining Champion status for his master, which he did in Wales at the

38 Sh. Ch. Tilehouse Tip, a border collie bred by the author and owned by Mr and Mrs Ross Green. *Photo*: Diane Pearce

Welsh Kennel Club Championships Show on 21 August, under Mrs Pru Green. Everyone who knows Buck and his sporting owners, Mary and Dusty Miller, were delighted at their eventual success and full of admiration for their endurance and dedication.

Even if a Show Champion border collie were to become a full champion under Kennel Club rules, having qualified by passing the sheep work test, such an exalted status can never outshine that of Supreme Sheepdog Champion on the trial field. When the champion's collar known as the Blue Ribbon of the Heather is placed around the neck of the winner for a performance in a role for which it was originally developed it will always make the winner king or queen of the border collies.

Besides my own contribution on the breed there are a number of other excellent books on these dogs in their role on the pastoral scene. The ISDS is the ruling body of the breed and there are now several clubs catering for the breed in the show or obedience rings.

20

The Fox Collie

References to fox collies crop up from to time, though frankly I have always been very sceptical about the existence of such an animal. Photographs of several of the early show collies looked remarkably like foxes, and were frequently described as of 'foxy appearance'. The breed standard laid down that 'fox colouring' was undesirable, so we can conclude that this colouring was distinct from the shades of sable which were becoming popular. Corgis are frequently described as having a foxy appearance.

Dogs described as fox collies are also mentioned as being one of the parents of some of the Australian breeds, and from time to time I get letters, mainly from Australia, asking what a fox collie is. More often the reference turns out to be only a description given to one particular dog, not a type or strain, but they merit some attention, even if it is only to satisfy our curiosity.

I am assured by eminent zoologists that from surveillance of dogs and foxes, kept under controlled conditions, matings have been observed, but there are no records of any live issue resulting from the union. However, live offsprings have resulted from a union between dogs and wolves, kept under the same conditions. This information, together with the numerous photographs I have been shown, has led me to the conclusion that the titles may possibly have referred to a purely local name for a type which has been useful for some purpose on the pastoral scene and resembled a fox either in colouring or cunning. In the same way, all over the British Isles, the same species of wild bird, wild animal or wild flower is recognized by a variety of names in different localities. I know that the common rabbit has at least six local names, and the hare and the robin also sport a few unusual titles in rural areas.

In Ireland farmers often kept, and still keep, a pup they call 'Foxy', usually the result of an accidental mating between a sheepdog and terrier, and if one or both parents displayed the sly cunning of a fox, then such a dog can be very useful for warding off Mr Reynard from poultry and for destroying small vermin.

A cross-bred can be more tractable than the wilful independent terrier, and less noisy. The same practice of cross-breeding was popular in Wales on remote farms, but there the dog was more likely to be a cross from a fox-coloured local herding variety like the popular hillman, 'foxy' being a popular name for any clever cross-bred.

An article written by a Mr Collins in 1781 on 'fox dogs' gives the following information which he said was supplied to him by a friend, a Mr Daniel.

> It was quite usual at that time in parts of northern England to tie up a bitch on heat in some remote woodland where a fox can have unrestricted access to her (lured by food set near), the offsprings were made esteemed for their usefulness in driving cattle, they bite keenly and are extensively active, playful and exceedingly expert at destroying rats, weasels and other vermin.

One is tempted to think that possibly the author had a type

like the Lancashire heeler in mind. Others flatly deny this, saying it is possible for a bitch tied up in this way to have been served by several dogs quite unobserved, and if crossed with a terrier the same usefulness and playful activity could apply.

The following little titbit comes from the *Irish Penny Magazine*, from which Edward Jesse gleaned most of the material for his *Anecdotes of Dogs* published in 1846: 'A woodman of the Manor of Mongewell in Oxfordshire owned a cur bitch which he declared was the offspring of a tame fox and a terrier bitch, yet she later bred to a common dog.' The editor of the magazine, it seems, took a keen interest in dogs and was considered something of an expert; he learned about this bitch when talking to the woodman while reporting on the progress of a royal hunting party in the district. I can only think that it made too good a story for a pressman to ignore!

Woodman, charcoal burners, warreners and foresters each kept a variety of dogs for a variety of reasons. Forest graziers kept a sort of collie cross something akin to a lurcher, and there are many tales of these having been crossed with a fox. It is quite possible that a bitch could stray away, and have been viewed while only being courted by a fox, but knowing the ways of foxes it is unlikely he would have pursued the matter much further, as they are too cunning to be held captive for any length of time while being unfaithful to the species, as when a 'tie' is effected. The bitch was much more likely to have been served unobserved by one or more of the other dogs in the vicinity. One never hears of a vixen mating with a dog, they are far too wise to be caught being unfaithful.

Sometimes an outstandingly clever or powerful animal can be produced by mixing different hereditary qualities, but these are often 'hybrids' and do not breed on true.

In the information supplied by Robert Kalaski from his book *Barkers and Biters* for the official publication of the Kennel Control Council, Victoria, *Dogs of Australia*, mention is made that the kelpie was developed from the fox collie imported from Scotland. Australian farming folk with whom I have corresponded in the past have told me that Robert Kalaski was a freelance journalist who frequently wrote articles for the farming journals, and they claim that these were quite often contradictory and not too well-informed. Certainly in his book *Dogs of the World* he gives us some extraordinarily contradictory information. In one chapter he declares that the border collie 'will not be nearly as successful a sheep worker as the smooth or fox-collie'. Later he goes on to state that

> as shown in previous articles, the setter owes its origin to the spaniel, which is naturally a timid dog, useful only for driving or retrieving birds and small game; therefore it lacks the compelling force which the descendants of the wild dog have over sheep, unless, as can be seen in some good strains of border collie, the setter has been almost bred out, and the fox or greyhound (descendant of the Indian red dog or dhole) has been bred in.

Elsewhere he claims the Sumatran red dog was the original fox dog – a sport – and that the original red dog of the world was the dingo. All very interesting, but very confusing, particularly as true collies would not have been known about at that period of time.

One further point which makes the importation of such a fox dog or collie into Australia very suspect, is the known fact that even if they had existed, then according to Mr Daniel, they were vicious and wild. If a dog of this nature were confined to a small space with little exercise for many weeks, as would have been the case on the long voyage to Australia, caring for them would have proved a dangerous if not an impossible duty for anyone in charge. Accommodation for animals on voyages in those days was not what it is today.

So let us turn to an equally thought-provoking aspect of this mysterious fellow. I have been told that in some areas of Wales and on Exmoor, where visibility is often poor, a dog with a special bark can be particularly useful in persuading scattered ewes and lambs to 'mother up'. In the past a dog which emitted a loud whining bark like a fox, was sometimes called a yodeller, and his frightening fox-like sound rang through the hills causing the wildly scattered grazing sheep to gather together for protection, thus making the work of the shepherd and dog much easier. The mating call of a vixen is a weird, spine-chilling sound, known in Ireland as the sound of the banshee, while the reply of the dog fox is not unlike yodelling. No doubt in remote areas these sound effects could be very effective, and a strange sound from even one dog in a valley could echo for miles through the mountains. The method of working of the huntaway, a herding dog recently imported into Britain from New Zealand, is a strong contestant in the noise stakes, and few can ignore those sounds emitted by a dog in love, which many owners will have experienced. Dogs that dislike the human singing voice, the piano or a violin, or are annoyed by the telephone bell, often resort to a throat noise quite distinct from howling.

One old farmer told me that after his father retired he trained his 'foxy' collie, with the aid of a piano and fiddle, to yodel, and in the evening the dog occasionally earned him extra money at a local music hall and many a pint in the pubs. I have seen a collie counting and yodelling in an act on the stage of the Coliseum in London, and my own collie is pretty useful at it when the phone rings!

The following is an extract from a report in the *Fancier's Gazette* of a dog show in Glasgow, in October, 1874.

> There was nothing in the Selling class, with the exception of Foxy, worth notice. Foxy is an interesting specimen of the Vulpo-canine cross, a hybrid but rarely seen; it appears

39 Golda, a fox collie owned by Mrs Ruth Hill

as good tempered and quiet as a lamb, though showing considerably more of the fox than the dog.

With so few authentic rural records it has been difficult to strike a balance between what are the facts and what is folklore, but whether these claims are true or false, this chapter should perhaps not be taken too seriously. However, it is worth putting on record, even for light relief, and certainly, whether any such vulpo-canine could be considered a serious contender as the ancestor of one of our modern breeds is open to question. The photograph reproduced here is of a dog of 'foxy' appearance said to resemble some of the old farm dogs of Wales, but in fact he is of very mixed ancestry, which goes to show that problems of identity are still with us. One of the dogs seen on the front of the book jacket would have been referred to as a fox collie in days gone by.

21

A New Status:
Demonstrations, Trials and Shows

The early history of sheepdog trials and dog shows has been re-corded many times, so here I propose only to recall the life-style of a select section of the community which had both the means and the desire to provide the right environment and the opportunity to foster and promote these leisure activities.

The International Sheepdog Society is often given the credit for developing trials, and indeed the Society has done a great deal for the shepherding world, but the seeds were sown, almost 100 years before its formation, in the soil of the big English country estates, where trials were nurtured through the nursery and kindergarten stages, to become established country events for the enjoyment of all sections of the com-munity.

The last quarter of the eighteenth century and the first quarter of the nineteenth saw many new reforms in the English way of life. Public benefactors who had previously patronized the arts were now turning their attention to the poor and needy. The great wealth created by the new industry contrasted with the poverty of the rural and suburban communities was becoming an embarrassment to Parliamentarians who rep-resented the people in rural areas, and also to a small section of wealthy benefactors.

Suddenly piety and self-indulgence were becoming less fashionable. New Parliamentary reforms, new attitudes to the teachings of the Church, in fact a new approach to religion, created a genuine concern and stimulated efforts to help the less fortunate, but the shepherd and his art came low on the list of those needing help, as indeed did farm labourers in general.

These reforms, in particular the Enclosure Acts, were not without hardship to the rural communities to begin with. The enclosure system applied to most of the country by 1830 and marked the end of the medieval peasant ownership of the countryside, the restriction of sheep walks and common free grazing, and the right to collect wood to keep the home fires burning. From the landowner's point of view it discouraged poaching game and desecrating good woodlands – both essential, not just for sport, but for victualling the labour force employed and housed on the estates. As a result good agricultural land could now be properly cultivated, and grazing more carefully controlled. In country terms these enclosed estates became known as the kingdom of the shepherd and this literally meant shepherds from either end of the social scale. I have given more details of this social distinction in an early chapter.

The Victorian era brought a somewhat different attitude to life and a different set of values. It was no longer considered in poor taste to brag or boast or to bring commerce into the social life of town or country. We were the great British Empire and proud of our achievements. The improving railway system was providing facilities for town folk to have easier access to country pursuits and for country folk to visit the big cities where the wealth was earned.

On the pastoral scene, sheep farming and livestock breeding were thriving and the ownership of land, wealth, good stock and experienced labour to care for it provided employment as well as income and sporting facilities. However, the occupation of shepherding was still a 'Cinderella art', in spite of the fact that new methods of livestock management and marketing being developed in New Zealand and Australia were the envy of the world. The shepherding world felt frustrated, and to our loss and their gain many self-employed shepherds from all over Britain emigrated to these far-flung parts of the Empire, to better their lot. Only when experienced shepherds were needed as replacements on the big estates in Britain did the scarcity become apparent. During that period wealthy landowners employed a huge labour force 'to keep up appearances', which indeed was a popular means of employment in an area where there were few opportunities to earn a living and accommodation was difficult, so the tithe cottage was a great blessing.

As we have seen, many English landowners also owned sporting properties in Scotland, Wales and Ireland, and it used to be said that the best-managed estates employed an English steward and gamekeeper, a Scottish shepherd and an Irish groom or stockman. (No doubt the Welshman stayed put to guard his territorial waters!) Large country house parties had long been great social and sporting occasions, and were also gradually becoming informal opportunities for relaxation for captains of industry or commerce, bankers and of course those connected with political life. The sport or entertainment provided by the host depended upon the tastes of the guests, the sporting facilities on the estate and the seasons of the year. Deer stalking, but not hunting or shooting, was compatible with the shepherd's way of life. The section of the community to which I refer includes the aristocracy, gentleman farmers or landed gentry and well-to-do yeoman farmers, lumped together by the Irish as 'the Ginthry set'.

A typical family which fitted perfectly into this social category were the Whitbreads of brewing fame. Samuel Whitbread, MP (1764–1815), was a successful businessman following in his father's footsteps at the London brewery. He was also a somewhat controversial figure in the Houses of

Parliament, but an admired and respected landowner and benefactor, and this was the kind of background typical of many of the big estate owners.

When they first married, Samuel and his wife lived at Woolmers, near Bedwell in Bedfordshire, which they later sold through Robert Dent, the brother of 'Dog' Dent, MP for Lancaster, the man who introduced the tax on dogs which is still in force. They then purchased Southill, which was one of the first estates to be enclosed. The miles of wall or fencing around most of the English stately homes still standing today bear witness to this system.

Succeeding sons each improved the estate and the home farm, especially in terms of sheep husbandry and sporting facilities. The first recorded field trial or demonstration was held at Southill in April 1865 and like all the early trials it was by invitation only. This glimpse into this particular life-style makes it easier to understand the circumstances which led up to a change of values in rural life, and the new status of a man and his dog.

Demonstrations

Forms of competition to test the abilities of working dogs, for entertainment or to settle an argument, had taken place for centuries when farm folk met to help each other out at certain seasons of the year, and were traditionally followed by celebrations. Later these occasions were known as 'collie gatherings', but as the beer flowed, the neglect and harsh treatment of the dogs increased, until clubs and societies were formed to run the events and to try to bring order to the proceedings and more regard for the dogs.

At local and county shows, parades, demonstrations or exhibitions of everything connected with rural life were very popular. View days or farm walks on the estates were regarded as dress rehearsals for these: they provided an opportunity for new suggestions to be put forward, and stock and labour alike benefited by being paraded before an audience. This was particularly helpful in the case of the shepherds' dogs as they rarely encountered a crowd of people with all the accompanying noises and bustle of a show, and sheepdog demonstrations were a very popular feature of the shows or fairs.

Regretfully I have no experience of social life in Wales, but in England and Ireland Sundays and Mondays were traditionally 'view days' on the estates, while Scotland of course observed the Sabbath. During the week huntsmen and gamekeepers, hounds and gun dogs provided the sport, but these two days were rest days, and it was the turn of the heads of other departments to parade the prize livestock or demonstrate the new machinery.

On Sundays, sandwiched sometime between church and lunch (usually at 3 or 4 o'clock), it was traditional for the host to take his guests on a conducted tour of the estate, while according to the season, the ladies went riding, walking, helped the hostess entertain the children, or toured the gardens. Head grooms dressed in smart livery and stable lads in clean white shirts lined up in front of the house with their magnificently turned out horses and carriages, sometimes even a donkey cart, for inspection and selection. The head gardener stood by to unlock the plant and stove house and show the ladies round, while on the home farm head stockmen in their Sunday best with shiny gaiters and brown bowlers or 'billy cocks', a new form of headgear denoting status, each paraded his prize-winning farm animal or demonstrated the latest machinery.

The 'billy cock' was an affectionate nickname for the low-fitting hard felt hat designed by William Coke in 1850 to replace the top hat, which tended to catch the wind, and to protect his own head and those of his gamekeepers from overhanging branches. It was made for him by T. and W. Bowler

(sometimes referred to as Beaulieu) of Southwark, and there-
after named the bowler or coke. Later these hats were issued to
all head keepers at Holkham Hall and at other estates and the
wearing of them became a mark of rank. In the well-known
painting of Coke inspecting his sheep before one of the famous
sheep shearings or 'Coke's Clippings', his head shepherd is
seen wearing one. The original colour was dark grey, then
brown came to be associated with horsemen, and the celebrated
brown derby was the correct headgear to wear for the Derby.
In time the wearing of a brown or grey or black bowler distinguished the county gentleman from the city gent, but it was
as protective headgear in the hunting field that it was most
popular, as an alternative to the top-hat at certain seasons. At
local and county shows, parades, or 'turn-outs' of horse-
drawn vehicles from local commercial undertakings were great
favourites with the public, and the traditional headgear was the
bowler, which it still is for stewards at a number of county
shows today.

Guests interested in the crops usually chose Mondays for
their tour, when venturing further afield beyond the farmyard
they finally reached the domain of the shepherd. The headherd,
as he was more usually called, would greet them resplendent in
his high-day smock of the traditional local colour and smock
patterning of the county, shiny boots and gaiters and a grey
bowler replacing the work-a-day shepherd's garb, with one or
two young dogs at his side. Naturally the Scottish shepherds
wore the shepherd's plaid and tam o'shanter. In Ireland
Sunday best was varied to say the least; the 'billy cock' was
sometimes worn, but was considered a sort of music hall joke
and perched usually at a very jaunty angle, greatly to the
annoyance of the English!

When grazing was short, sheep at that time were kept in folds
and fed turnips, or swedes as they became known, a form of
management introduced by the Cokes of Norfolk; so a dif-

ferent type of dog was needed to those of the hill shepherds. The lighter-boned 'eye' dog was becoming fashionable, and in fact the old bobtail was still used quite a lot on farms. When flock management and improvements had been discussed with host and guests, the shepherd would give a demonstration with his dogs. These belonged to the shepherd, not the landlord, and these demonstrations helped to show off their potential, should the select audience need new stock dogs.

Guests from overseas were always particularly delighted by these demonstrations as they greatly admired the intelligence and stamina of our herding dogs. Many brought their own shooting dogs with them, there being no rabies restrictions in those days, and with the help of a little palm-greasing the opportunity was often taken to cross one of the shepherd's dogs with one of the foreign dogs in the hope of improving any deficiencies. It is said that the great improvement in the Brittany spaniel was due to just such a cross, and the offspring were also found to be very useful in the folds, just as in another area borzois had been crossed with shepherds' dogs to improve stamina and trainability.

A cross between a gun dog and collie which was alleged to have taken place somewhere about 1826 gained a great deal of adverse publicity. It concerned the Marquis of Huntley, a somewhat unpopular sportsman in his day, who persuaded a local shepherd-cum-part-time gamekeeper, who lived close to Findhorn and owned a very clever collie called Maddy – as good at poaching game as she was at herding – to mate her with one of his setters in an effort to improve the nose and intelligence of the breed. The incident rubbed salt into the wounds of the Irish setter breeders who at the time were suffering from their dogs' reputation for being beautiful but brainless and difficult to train, and therefore with distinct limitations except in the best hands.

In 1830, after he had succeeded to the title of the Cock of the

North or the 4th Duke of Gordon, His Grace was publicly proclaiming that the line he was now breeding were a distinct breed to be known as the Castle Gordon setters. However, demonstrations of their new qualities did not match up to his boastings about the spectacular performances of those offspring, which were considered in such bad taste that they provoked a great deal of controversy, and a Mr C. F. Bastin and other contemporary well-known gundog breeders wrote many letters to *The Times* and *The Field* strongly denying the Duke's claims.

In spite of the controversy – or perhaps because of it – the Duke brought eleven so-called Castle Gordon setters to Tattersalls in London that year for sale by auction. The price of 72 guineas was paid for a black, white and tan dog named Young Regent and said to resemble a collie; two pups of twelve weeks old sold for 15 guineas each, and a black-and-tan dog said to resemble a setter fetched 34 guineas; these were exorbitant prices to pay for a dog in those days.

Trials

Early trials, like the early dog shows, were for gun dogs only, and a selling class was always included in the day's events. Many of the overseas sportsmen preferred to buy and keep a dog in this country, the quality of our dogs and the skills of our trainers being regarded as second to none.

Field trials had been held annually in England since 1865, and in Wales those held on the Rhiwlas estate near Bala since 1867 had grown from one to two day events. Estate workers were expected to help each other out at busy seasons of the year, in fact they enjoyed the break from their own routine, especially going out with guns in the shooting season as it earned a few tips, but when it came to the holding of gun dog or field trials it interfered with the shepherd's daily work with his flocks, as the trials also entailed mustering all the estate labour that could be spared to run the trials.

The Australasian carrot was still dangling, and so good relations between shepherds and landowners were even more important now than in the past. It occurred to several members of the landed gentry and to yeoman farmers who owned estates with sporting facilities and who also employed shepherds, that the 'view day' private demonstrations did not give the shepherds and their dogs the recognition they deserved and that some form of organized demonstration, which the public could attend, was desirable.

When plans for the 1873 field trials at Bala were being

40 The first sheepdog trials at Bala in 1873. Sketch from
London Graphic, 1874. The dog in the foreground is
believed to be Bess, mother of Trefoil

discussed it was decided by the organizers, Mr S. E. Shirley, Mr F. Parmeter, Mr T. Ellis and Mr Richard Lloyd Price, on whose Rhiwlas estate the trials were to be held, to extend the event one further day and hold a trial for shepherds and their dogs. The venue was considered suitable, sheep were available and all the facilities for a public event would already be *in situ*. Mr. Shirley offered to bring over his shepherds and his dogs from Ireland to help with the sheep needed for the trial, and there were many other offers of help.

In fact it was Mr Shirley who masterminded the trial; he was a great believer in good relations between the families in the 'big house' and the families of the estate workers of all ranks. The dog fraternity owe a great deal to this remarkable young man, for he founded the Kennel Club in the same year, at the age of only twenty-nine. We shall return to him later.

In horse trials or racing, the skill and physical fitness of the rider is just as important to the end result as the suitability, fitness and training of the animal, but should horse and pilot be parted during the set course, then the partnership is broken. At sheepdog trials skill, fitness and experience are also needed, but above all trust, for pilot and animal are parted at the start of the course, and from then on the partnership is guided by a sort of radio link or remote control instrument called a whistle, although some say it is really telepathy.

At sheepdog trials the pilot is called a handler, be he novice or old hand, and the villains of the piece are the sheep, those awkward creatures who on being released from a pen, and finding themselves in a strange situation without their usual leader, frequently revert to all their wild instincts. This is where real experience in shepherding counts, to balance the situation and get back on course.

As a spectator sport modern sheepdog trials, especially national events, have become popular family events, and as a leisure pursuit they have captured the imagination of many dog owners who, as a result of watching the events in close-up on television, imagine themselves to be budding shepherds. Hobby herding, as some call it, is a comparatively new form of leisure pursuit, taken up by men and women from all walks of life. Those who own a herding dog which they feel, or have been told, has the potential to perform the task for which it was originally bred, but who do not have the facilities for training or testing on livestock, will go to great lengths to find ways of satisfying this urge. Having mastered the 'art', those who own stock, but previously lacked the ability to train a stock dog, may now be content simply to put it to the test at home, but those with the competitive spirit will become more adventurous and want to test their new-found skill and partnership by entering for a local trial; and a number have had great success from this approach and gone on to win at bigger events.

There are at the present time so many accomplished 'hobby-herders' competing at the small trials that the full-time shepherds sometimes have to look to their laurels when competing against them. However, it is more often the experienced professional shepherds or true herdsmen who walk off with the top awards. From their knowledge of the ways of sheep they can often anticipate the reactions of a certain breed in a given situation and direct the dog accordingly.

Today almost all forms of dog or horse trials can be labelled spectator sports or leisure pursuits and many are commercially sponsored. There is no denying the rewards and benefit which owners of top winners receive from these events, but anyone who believes that modern sheepdog trials still completely fulfil their original purpose must be living in cloud cuckoo land.

Shows

Dog showing is a contentious subject, and perhaps not

everyone will even agree with the move to found the Kennel Club, but when one acknowledges that exhibitions of this nature, once established, were not only here to stay (as has been proved) but in the early days were riddled with every sort of skulduggery, one will realize the debt owed to Servallis Evelyn Shirley who strove to make it a respectable sport. The Shirleys can trace their ancestry back to the Domesday Book and there is a thriving Shirley Society in America.

Servallis Evelyn Shirley was born in 1844, and after his father's death he took over the running of Ettington Park (Ettington Park is now a luxury hotel and has retained many of the Shirley treasures) estate near Stratford-upon-Avon at a very early age. He was later appointed a Justice of the Peace. He continued for some time to breed his father's famous Shirley retrievers, which are now known as flat-coated retrievers. Being a first-class shot, he knew the requirements of a good gun dog, hence his great interests in field trials. The Shirleys also owned a magnificent house and farm in County Monaghan in Ireland, and from 1868 to 1880 he represented the county in Parliament. Mr Shirley was also a very fine horseman and owned and hunted a pack of harriers which were kennelled at Lough Fea Carrigmacross, his Irish home.

It was from Lough Fea that he brought over his shepherd, Mr Smith, and two of his collies, a dog and a bitch, to help with the sheep needed for the 1873 trials. The ancestry of all the modern rough-coated show collies can be traced back to these two collies, but their story belongs in the history of the breed. I am most grateful to Mr Shirley's grandson, Major John Shirley, for filling me in on many interesting aspects of this great man.

The history of trials and shows would not be complete without recording the part Mr Shirley played in promoting the collie for the enjoyment of all, and here are extracts written as a tribute by Mr E. W. Jaquet, the secretary of the Kennel Club at the time of his death in 1904, which I think sum up the whole

41 Portrait by Stuart Wortley of Mr S. E. Shirley, MP, JP, founder of the Kennel Club in 1873 and 'father' of our modern show collies. Pictured here with one of the famous Shirley flat-coated retrievers. *Photo*: Major John Shirley

show scene of the period and in particular Mr Shirley's contribution to it.

> In the interval of fourteen years between the date of the
> first dog show and the foundation of the KC many
> irregularities – not to say scandals – had arisen and the need
> for legislation and guidance became an absolute necessity.
> ... No doubt Mr Shirley's intimate knowledge of canine
> matters of those days had led him, long before he took
> public action, to perceive that unless a responsible
> authority took affairs in hand, dog showing and breeding
> must eventually become a pursuit in which no respectable
> person would care to engage. . . . It is solely owing to the
> influence of the Club that today dog breeding and dog
> showing are pursuits which can be indulged in by
> gentlewomen.

The first dog show held in Newcastle upon Tyne in June,
1859, was confined to pointers and setters. Although there
were a number of exhibits, the judge for pointers took first
prize of a pair of shot guns with his setters, while the judge of
setters did likewise with his pointers. The guns were presented
to a Mr W. R. Pape who was very interested in organizing the
show and was head of the famous gunsmiths' establishment in
the city. This goes to show that even the judges were a little
suspect in their behaviour in the early days.

In 1860, at the Birmingham show, sheepdogs, or colleys,
yard dogs or keeper's dogs were scheduled, and it was the re-
sponsibility of the owner to state the breed or strain of the
exhibit. As can be seen in the Kennel Club Stud Book records,
the variety of the strains or breed titles claimed for some
exhibits in the non-sporting section was mind-boggling, as was
the variety of colours given in the descriptions of the exhibits.

In the early days of shows, pedigrees were of little consequence, and even the breed of the exhibit was often defined in

vague terms. Most of the dogs were shown by gamekeepers, kennel staff or shepherds employed on the owners' estate, who took more interest in the performance of their charges than in their looks, but following on from field trials, these new indoor events gave added interest and incentive to employees and became very popular.

All forms of shows and trials brought the working dog into public view and attendance at both events was a social occasion. As we have seen, with the interest of royalty in these events, and in particular Queen Victoria's love of the shepherd's dogs, their popularity soared and the humble herding dog was granted a new status, and many breeds of dogs were exhibited by members of the royal family in person.

Breeds of dog originally entered on the Kennel Club register fell into two groups, sporting and non-sporting, but as more and more breeds were registered it became necessary to extend the group system, until today we have six groups, Hounds, Gundogs, Terriers, Utility, Toy and Working: the herding or pastoral breeds come into the last group. Almost every year a foreign herding breed is added to what is now such a huge group that I would hazard a guess that it will not be long before it is found necessary to have a separate herding group.

The Kennel Club requires every dog competing under its rules and regulations to be registered there under its recognized or fixed pure breed. Subsequently with the institution of the Stud Book, the pedigree and show awards of every registered dog are recorded here. In recent years the number of registered dogs has increased to such an extent that qualification for entry into the Stud Book has had to be limited to wins in higher classes.

Between 1873 and 1877 Champion classes were provided at dog shows held under the rules of the Kennel Club, and many owners claimed their dogs were champions if they had won a first prize in these classes. Then in 1877 the Kennel Club decided that the title of Champion could not be assumed until a dog had won three first prizes, although it did not specify any particular shows or classes. In 1880 this was amended to four first prizes, one of which had to be won at the Birmingham Show.

Today the title of Full Champion can only be claimed if a dog has won three Challenge Certificates under three different judges, at least one of which must be after the dog is twelve months old. A border collie can only be called a Show Champion under these rules, unless it has passed a special working test on stock or has won an award at a sheepdog trial run under International Sheep Dog Society rules. The Society is the governing body of the sheepdog world, and registrations and stud book entries are only accepted from members; all dogs are registered as working sheepdogs – the Society is not concerned with breed points – but if owners wish to exhibit an ISDS-registered dog in the showring, it must also be registered at the Kennel Club.

It can be seen that the introduction of dog shows, field or sheepdog trials, and dogs trained to exhibit other forms of useful work, opened up a whole new arena for dog owners. It was generally welcomed by all involved as it created a new interest and much needed employment, but above all it created a new status for the herdsman's dog. Later, other new roles in which to exploit his instincts and intelligence were created by obedience, working and agility tests.

Understandably, to those who work with these dogs as part of their livelihood and use them for their original purpose, some aspect of this new status is abhorrent. However, these new forms of competition provide the answer to those owners who admire the herding breeds and wish to further their interest in dog ownership and stimulate their dogs' brains, but do not have the facilities to use them for their original purpose either for work or sport. They certainly provide a great deal of pleasure, and the free choice of participation in either world remains with the owners.

The popularity of dog shows and allied Kennel Club events is evident by the increase of exhibits every year since the first dog show was held in 1859. At the Ladies' Kennel Association show in 1984, a total of 14,611 dogs were exhibited over the two days of the show. At Cruft's in 1985 no less than 11,141 dogs were entered over the three days of the show, and each dog has to qualify for entry by winning a first prize at a Championship Show held during the previous year, or be a full Champion. The Kennel Club was forced to impose this restriction due to overwhelming numbers of owners who wished to enter their dogs. In 1986 this restriction was amended to allow dogs entered in the Kennel Club Stud Book to compete.

Some call the breeds in the showring 'manufactured breeds', but I prefer to think of them as the product of selective breeding from good pure strains. Unfortunately at times, as with everything else, the whims and fancies of fashion have a strong influence in altering the original picture.

Bibliography

Barrington, John, *Red Sky at Night*, Pan Books 1984
Baskerville, W., *Show Collies and Shetland Sheepdogs*, 'Our Dogs' Publishing Co. Ltd. No date given
Billingham, Viv, *One Woman and her Dog*, Patrick Stephens 1984
Bishop, Ada, *All about the Collie*, Pelham Books 1971
Combe, Iris, *Border Collies*, Faber and Faber 1978
Combe, Iris, *Shepherds, Sheep and Sheepdogs*, Dalesman 1983
Girouard, Mark, *Life in the English Country House*, Yale University Press, 1978
Gosset, A. L. J, *Shepherds of Britain*, Constable 1911
Gould, J., *The Old English Sheepdog*, Pelham Books 1973
Halsall, Eric, *Sheepdogs, my Faithful Friends*, Patrick Stephens 1980
Halsall, Eric, *Sheepdog Trials*, Patrick Stephens 1982
Holmes, John, *The Farmer's Dog*, Popular Dogs 1960
Hubbard, C., *Working Dogs of the World*, Sidgwick & Jackson 1947
Jesse, George R., *Researches into the History of British Dogs*, Robert Hardwick 1866
Kaleski, Robert, *Australian Barkers and Biters*, Endeavour Press 1933

Keay, John, *Highland Drove*, John Murray 1984

Lee, Rawdon B., *The Collie or Sheepdog*, Horace Cox 1980

Leighton, *The Book of the Dog*, Cassell 1907

Longton and Hart, *The Sheepdog, his Work and Training*, David and Charles 1969

McCulloch, J. Herries, *Sheepdogs and their Masters*, Dinwiddie 1938

Osborne, Margaret, *The Collie*, Popular Dogs 1957

Osborne, Margaret, *The Shetland Sheepdog*, Popular Dogs 1959, 1967

Quarton, Margaret, *The Working Border Collie*, Pelham Books 1986

Rogers, Byron, *Drovers Trail, Sunday Telegraph Magazine* 1984

Vesey-Fitzgerald, Brian, *The Domestic Dog*, Routledge & Kegan Paul 1957

Vidler, Peidje, *The Border Collie in Australasia*, Australia 1983

Willison, G. O., *The Bearded Collie*, Foyles 1971

Youatt, William, *Cattle and their Management*, Longmans, Green & Co. 1886

Youatt, William, *Sheep and their Management*, Longmans, Green & Co. 1864

Youatt, William, *The Dog*, Longmans, Green & Co. 1879

Various contributors, *Dogs, their Points, Whims, Instincts, Peculiarities*, Dent 1874

Index

Page numbers in *italic* refer to the illustrations

Index